GIANT TALES

DANGEROUS DAYS

CRYSTAL SWORD CHRONICLES:

GRYFFON MASTER

GIANT TALES
3-MINUTE STORIES

DANGEROUS
DAYS

Introduction by
PROFESSOR
K.R. LIMN

Professor Limn Books
Charlotte, North Carolina

DEDICATION

For Anna who enjoys reading fiction

Preface

Giant Tales: Dangerous Days (Book 4)
will take you to another world
where the forecast calls for hot days.
We will take a look at how
characters are responding to
powerful women and mysterious crowns.

I am delighted to present
fifty-three giant tales in
four chapters of reading entertainment:
One Hot Day, Dangerous Days,
Crowns, and Another World.

PROFESSOR K.R. LIMN

writers750.com

Contents

CHAPTER ONE
ONE HOT DAY

CHAPTER TWO
DANGEROUS DAYS

CHAPTER THREE
CROWNS

CHAPTER FOUR
ANOTHER WORLD

AFTERWORD

Joyce Shaughnessy

Tom Russell

Andy McKell

Todd Folstad

Randall Lemon

Sylvia Stein

Arlene Lagos

Mike Boggia

Glenda Reynolds

J.R. O'Neill

H.M. Schuldt

Gene Hilgreen

Mirta Oliva

Alli Vaughan

Lynette White

Connie Flanagan

Neil Carroll Ellison

D C Mills

David Russell

Rebecca Lacy

Karen Beck

Shelly Heskett Harris

Lynn Johnston

Mary Agrusa

Karen Hopkins

A.A. Abbott

Craig Teal

Shae Hamrick

Victor J.M. Christensen

Tim Girard

Elaine Faber

Randy Dutton

INTRODUCTION

In July of 2013, authors were asked to write a short story with three highlights: a super hot day, a superstition, and something to do with liberty. The top three winning stories from the JULY HEAT contest were third place winner *All In A Day's Work* by Dorthe Moller Christensen, second place winner *Sack* by Alli Vaughan, and first place winner *The Blessing Way* by Joyce Shaughnessy.

In November of 2013, authors were given another challenge to write a short story, but this time with the following three highlights: a crown, a window, and a powerful woman. Top winning stories from the NOVEMBER CROWNS contest include *More Than Just Window Dressing* by Connie Flanagan, *Forsake Thy Bloodline* by Alli Vaughan, and *Cassie's Crown* by Lynn Johnston.

The short stories in this anthology, *Giant Tales: Dangerous Days (Book 4)*, are fictional. Without any further ado, I invite you to sit back, relax, and enjoy 53 tales of hot days, powerful women, and mysterious crowns.

PROFESSOR K.R. LIMN

DANGEROUS DAYS

CHAPTER ONE
ONE HOT DAY

1

THE BLESSING WAY

by

Joyce Shaughnessy

As she stepped out on the deck, Kate could see the enormous fire covering the horizon. The blaze was so close to her house that she could feel the intense heat and hear the crackling of the huge inferno. Her long, silky black hair was pulled in the back and tied with a leather string in which rested a single eagle feather.

Tears of sadness rolled down her high cheekbones as she witnessed the destruction of the land handed down for generations by her Navajo tribe. The dry pine trees only added fuel to the inferno. Kate Eagle Feather was known as a Yenene or "healer" among her tribe. Her ancestors had been well-respected medicine men and women, and as such, they possessed mystical powers.

Kate walked into the house and put her arm around her daughter. Nuna was only eight but understood what the fires meant. She knew she'd never return to this house again, but she didn't mourn it the way her Mama did. There would always be room for them in someone else's home, because they were all of the same Navajo family.

Last night, Kate had seen a black raven looking directly at her and heard a rooster crow. Both signs meant death was near. Somehow she needed to show Nuna the *Blessing Way*, the return to harmony between nature and Mother Earth unsettled by drought and hot conditions.

Kate looked up and saw a small house in the corner of the room. It was surrounded by burning fire, and she fell onto her knees, lost in time and reality. As she stared at the vision, strange men with torches appeared, and Kate saw her own body bound by ropes, being held captive. The men were yelling, "Devil! Witch!"

Kate instinctively knew what it meant. This was her past, when people outside her world hadn't understood the healing powers she possessed. She had heard tales about it all her life—how people had burned healers at the stake, because they believed they were possessed by the devil. She felt that this vision meant that she must sacrifice her own life in order to return harmony to her world, but for now she had to consider Nuna. What would happen to her? She put her head in her hands.

"Mama, what do you see now?"

"I see death, Nuna."

"Whose death, Mama?"

Still seeing the vision before her, she answered, "Mine."

There was a forceful knock on the door, and the vision disappeared. Kate answered the door, and a trooper was there. "You need to leave, ma'am."

"We were just leaving."

The trooper nodded and left.

Kate turned and said, "Nuna, do you have everything you want? Your teddy?"

"Yes, ma'am." Tears were welling up in her eyes. "Are you going to die, Mama?"

"No, sweetheart. Not yet at least. Let's go.

Once in the car, Kate stopped at the end of the driveway and stared at the only house she had known her entire life. She knew that in an hour or so, the fire would be eating away at the roof.

When they arrived at the Council House, Kate noticed everyone was there except their Council Chief, Tom Running Water.

Kate asked Mary, "Where's Tom?"

"I have no idea. I talked to him earlier this morning and he said he was loading his Jeep. He should have been here by now."

"Has anyone tried to call him since then?"

"Yes, but there was no answer."

Kate said, "I'm going to check on him. Nuna, you stay close to the others."

Nuna replied, "Be careful, Mama," still nervous about the vision.

"Don't worry, sweetheart. I'll be careful. I just need to check on Tom." She knew from her vision this morning that her purpose was somehow connected to finding Tom.

Kate was met with a burning house when she reached Tom's. She jumped out of the car and ran toward it yelling, "Tom! Tom, it's Kate!"

Two firefighters ran up to her, and she frantically asked, "Where's Tom? He lives here by himself."

One of them said, "Don't know. You need to leave right now for your own safety!"

"I can't. I have no choice."

Kate ran back to her car and grabbed a blanket to cover her body. She ran for the garage, hoping to find Tom still alive.

"Tom! Tom!"

She could barely see anything but fire and smoke. She ran inside and saw him lying on a step in his house. "Tom, get up! Get up!"

Kate was coughing uncontrollably, inhaling smoke when she reached him. Trying to stay as close to the ground as possible, she dragged him across the floor. As she reached the garage door, the firemen ran to them and took them to paramedics.

After she was satisfied that Tom was okay and she was able to see, Kate looked up and saw a lone eagle sitting at the very edge of the burning forest.

Why? He would know better than to come here. Then she realized that he was there for a purpose. Seeing an eagle meant luck, a savior. She knew why. It was there as a sign—that she had brought all of them through the *Blessing Way* into life.

Kate couldn't wait to see Nuna. They had a life now. They had come through the burning fire.

An afterword to this story is on page 209.

2

FLYING LIBERTY

by

Tom Russell

A periscope nudged dirt and dust from the baked orange soil and remained still for a moment. Slowly, the dull silver tube began to turn ever so slowly, scanning the horizon—for what—that was the question. After a few rotations, the periscope descended and the dirt and dust returned.

Jordan Rivers was an engineer, a wealthy engineer who many of his peers believed was overzealous in his superstitions. In his office hanging on his wall was a chart that hung like a calendar with weather patterns and temperature fluctuations dating back to the year 2050, fifteen years ago. Rivers could see a pattern developing.

"Your house is paid for. Why on earth would you ever consider selling your house, especially at such an incredibly low price?" questioned the pretty real estate agent as she eyed Rivers carefully. "

"Just get the paperwork done," he told her.

Buying land with a deep underground well wasn't a problem. The land located near the mountains was secluded. The site that Rivers had chosen offered a view of all four directions, but was in a location that was fairly difficult to get to. The digging began by an excavator from another state who dug up the still moist soil to a depth of sixty feet. Once the pit was complete, Rivers began construction of a structure that was to become his home.

It happened quickly, brought on by a solar flare that raged for days. The ice caps in the Arctic melted so fast that the oceans filled and overflowed onto the flat of the lands. The land began to lose the colors of life as a reddish-brown tint overtook the ground where lush green grass once lay.

Rivers had stocked his shelter with enough food and water to last for many years. He had enough entertainment and gadgets producing electricity to be comfortable. He had built his house precisely to fit his needs and the needs of his companion Nancy, who was the only person who believed what he was trying to tell everyone—that the world was dying.

Nearly everything above ground burned. The heat from the solar flare caught nearly everyone off-guard. There were a few people that Rivers had thought would survive, like miners and others living in underground bunkers or caves. But without a steady supply of food and water, it was unlikely very many would last for more than a month.

"Why didn't they want to believe me?" he said as he surveyed the sensors monitoring a lifeless landscape. "But there's always hope."

As the days rolled into months and the months into years, the resiliency of Earth began when rays of sunlight managed to cut through the haze of smoky grayness. The volcanoes that had long ago spewed ash and destruction roared into silence. The animals that lived underground were becoming restless as they scurried about, leaving the freshest of footprints on land after nature left long ago to fend for itself.

Rivers checked the sensors again and marked the data onto the sheet of paper tacked to a nearby wall.

"I'll give it another month, then I'll go outside," he said as he walked down the hallway to check on Nancy who was nine months pregnant.

"I'm dilating," she whispered. Her voice trembled with a hushed excitement. "Your baby's ready to come out."

Rivers prepared the delivery room and wheeled Nancy into the clean sterilized room. Within a few hours, a cry echoed down the hall as Rivers wrapped his daughter in a fresh comforter and placed her on Nancy's chest.

"She's healthy," beamed Rivers who couldn't take his eyes off of her. "Look at her wings. I hope they can carry her far."

Jordan Rivers, the famed bio-engineer, had done it. He managed to keep his bloodline alive. He did it his way to change the course of history. His children would fly and their children would fly. His daughter, whom he named Liberty, was beautiful.

An afterword to this story is on page 210.

3

IN OTHER HANDS

by
Andy McKell

When she woke, she was in her own bed in her own room in her own home; she was sure of that. But somehow—something—was not right. There was an odd light shining from just beyond her field of vision. And two children stood in the shadows near her feet.

Children? No, not children. She knew them for what they were. Short, dressed in snug, grey lab suits. How did she know they were lab suits? How did she know that they wore lab helmets, domed and fitted with black, oval lenses? How did she know that these creatures were called "Greys"? She was confused. She knew these things, as if from a dream or a dim memory, but did not know how she knew.

They stood waiting, as if with infinite patience. She was unaware of their conversation, had no means to detect it or to participate in it. She tried to call out to them, to raise an arm, to sit up. She tried; she failed. She was immobile. This was familiar. Then she began to remember something.

Beyond the walls of this place that was her room, but was not her room, two other creatures observed. Their bodies shone as if composed of light and fire. From their tall, almost skeletal frames, it seemed that a random drapery of ragged cloth fluttered, flame like. The tatters flickered behind them, as if they faced forever into some unperceived wind that affected nothing and no-one else. Only a part of them existed in the physical plane.

The smaller of the two, whose light was the less glorious, turned its head, communicating without sound. "Master, the procedure is complete. The subject is awake."

"Novice, you may join me for the learning."

They moved, glided, into the airlock that separated their control room from the earth-environment laboratory. They steeled themselves for the rush of air. Their glowings stuttered; their stick-thin bodies bent forward in sudden agony; they vanished; they reappeared. Slowly, their lights grew to flare once more, but with a diminished glory.

"Carbon dioxide!" The Master's distaste ran as a dark undercurrent to the thought. "Your first taste of toxic gas. Learn well how it corrodes our link with the physical world, as it does the creatures below. And it grows daily more concentrated. They cannot endure for many more generations. We must work faster to complete the Earth Project and withdraw."

The Novice signaled understanding. They paused for a while, recovering and acclimating, before entering the lab. It seemed to the woman that they emerged from the flower-patterned decoration on her wall, flooding the room with a glare that stung her eyes. The Greys, protected by their visor lenses, bowed slightly. She tried to blink. She could not blink. She tried to call out. She could not call out.

Deep inside her, she was aware of sounds shaped like words. "Have no fear. Think to me. Do you remember us?"

She felt a joy rising inside her, overcoming her fear. "Y-yes!" She thought it without thinking to think. She was confused, but she did know these creatures. She had been here before. Many times.

The Master ran the tests, checking that she was unharmed by the procedure. She endured without fear, but not without some distress, despite the sedating resonances. Satisfied, it waited for her inevitable questions. The subjects always asked the same questions. It was good that they sought to reach beyond their grasp.

"Please tell me. Why am I here? What have you done to me?" Always the same questions.

Impatience was as alien to this creature of light as these beings were to the human. The Master explained, truthfully, but in very simple terms.

The Novice was curious. "Do you always tell them these things? We erase their memories of the visit, so what is the purpose?"

"Because it calms and reassures. Erasure is not total. We seek to encourage confidence that we are not hostile, that we are kind and caring. It does not always work; sometimes they retain fear and confusion. But we intend to reduce distress for when they are summoned again to continue the procedures. That is why we now simulate their private enclaves, as they were afraid of the laboratory. Why deny them consolation? And why tell a lie, if they do not remember?"

"Master, are we certain that they will never detect our tinkering with their DNA?"

"We are using their own genetic material, modifying the sequences, enhancing existing potential that lies dormant. It is undetectable."

Later, once again glowing fully in their safe environment, they gazed through the viewing panel at the blue and white planet rolling through space below their craft. The Master continued to explain to the Novice.

"As they begin to succumb to the toxic gas and the heat, our enhancements will lead to accelerated evolutionary change. They will quickly breed a race of humans that can thrive at higher carbon-dioxide levels and at higher surface temperatures.

"The plant life, of course, will flourish naturally in higher concentrations of the gas. Food will become abundant. Humanity has a good, potential future." Caution coloured the pronouncement. Nothing was certain.

They considered the vast array of laboratories within the undetectable hulls of the orbiting fleet. They were as factories, seizing, modifying and returning untold numbers of creatures engineered to survive better in the coming ages of the Earth.

"We can provide only a second chance for these humans. The rest is in their own hands."

An afterword to this story is on page 211.

ALPHA LAMPUS

by
Todd Folstad

Well, it's Christmas time again, July 15, the mid-point of the year when we all hail our great leader and pay homage to him in tribute for all he has done for us. This is the 53rd celebration of Christmas here on AL4, and it has been the hottest and darkest of years.

Today the sun is cooking us down at forty degrees Celsius. The plague was born in such a year, and now that it's gone, we are only left with the heat. AL4 has been steadily getting hotter for the past half-century, and we are only now working on ways to cool our homes and produce new ways to shield us from its blazing, searing assault.

Back in '60, when the plague had finished ravaging our little place in the sky, he was the one who provided a direction, a path to follow, an initiative to implement. We were in desperate times and truly needed a leader to tell us what we had to do to survive, to thrive and to begin again. He was that man.

St. Nicholas, a refugee from a far-off planet, became a healer who had a natural immunity to our plague and freely shared by creating a vaccine. He almost came too late as the planetary population was down to less than 1,000 people, barely a viable pool to repopulate this barren world. He brought new ideas, new thoughts on how we could achieve growth and re-birth. All that was required was that we follow him without question. He would become our new emperor, our new god and savior. All we had to do was accept him.

Before he came, we didn't have many options, so a vote was taken. With less than two percent of the population against it, we, in essence, sold our souls to this red and white devil. What we didn't know, would come to haunt our present and future for untold generations.

He came from a place where greed and avarice—foreign concepts to us—were the everyday norm. People there didn't work for the good of all, they worked for more things to possess. As he tells it, it was a market economy, where he who has the most is the leader. When he arrived, we needed what he had, and since he had the most, we were beholden to him. If only we could have found a way to save ourselves, how much different our world would be today. How much more freedom and self-ownership we might have.

The children were the first to fall under his spell as they enjoyed the toys, games, and diversions that he brought them—ways to separate them from us and the community. We should have seen what was happening, but with the plague beaten back and life returning to AL4, we were just happy to be alive and growing again. We were fools.

He began opening factories to produce the instruments of our own enslavement, which employed all who needed work, including the children, who were the most eager of all. They loved working for "Nick," as he asked them to call him, so they could see the toys before they became available to all.

As they aged, the children were made part of the greater society, first as guardians, then later enforcers of "Nick" and his army of enforcers.

So I've told how the toys and games culled the masses, but the most insidious items were the use of green trees and baubles called ornaments, in the homes of citizens to show obedience to "Nick."

Worst of all were the red and white clothing items worn by our leader and his enforcers. Gaudy, fluffy, furry suits and pants with thick black belts that they used for whipping the disobedient into compliance. Heavy black boots that they used to crush the hands, feet, and occasionally heads of the heretics. It was as I've said, a dark time.

From where in the universe could this monster have been spawned? Is there really such a place that he could have come from where this lifestyle is flourishing? I pray for the future of our planet and our people that there will be a new savior to come along and bring peace and happiness back to AL4. Until then, we wait, watch, and comply...*Un-Silent Night, Un-Holy Night, All is Not Calm, All is Not Bright.*

An afterword to this story is on page 212.

5

TAKING LIBERTIES

by

Randall Lemon

Barbie looked out the window of her pink Malibu mansion but the landscape had drastically changed. No longer did she see her perfectly blue kidney-shaped pool. No longer did she see the waves of the blue Pacific lapping gently at the golden sands of Southern California.

Now what Barbie viewed from her window was desolate and alien. How would Ken ever find her now and pick her up in the pink convertible for their surfing date? They had planned this weekend together for a long time. Barbie's annoying kid sister, Skipper, was going to be away at summer camp with all the little other plastic sisters and sidekicks and she and Ken could be alone together at last.

But now there was no surf, no ocean, no Ken. Skipper had been playing with Barbie's makeup (as usual) and left her gilded hand mirror right at the edge of the sink. After Skipper had been picked up by the camp bus, Barbie had rushed into the bathroom to do her hair and makeup to make herself (even more) beautiful for Ken. Unfortunately, she hadn't noticed the mirror hanging so precariously over the sink's edge. She swept past it with her perfectly proportioned hip and knocked it to the floor. It hit the pink tiles and smashed into a thousand pieces.

"Oh drat! There's seven years bad luck," said Barbie.

She quickly covered her mouth with her hand. Had she really cursed? Barbie couldn't believe what she had said. "I should wash my mouth out with pink soap," said Barbie.

But Barbie's problems extended far beyond a simple curse word. For later she had looked outside and realized that her luck was so bad, that somehow her house had been transported to a landscape that seemed more appropriate to the planet Mercury. She had no cool pink swimming pool filled with clear blue water and the ocean also seemed to have disappeared.

The blinding sun stood huge and low in the sky. Some of Barbie's patio furniture had already begun to melt from the extreme heat. Barbie started to panic. She had always heard about things like global warming, although the concept had always seemed a little too intellectual for Barbie to truly grasp.

Luckily her boyfriend, Ken, was quite an intelligent guy and had explained it to Barbie in simple terms: "Globe is the big ball we live on, and warming means it gets hotter, so global warming means we get more hot air and less cold air, I guess."

I admire Ken so much, Barbie thought, *If only we had anatomically correct parts, we could have children as smart as him and as beautiful as me!*

Just then, Barbie started to note that a hole had started forming in one of her plastic walls. She also noted that her beautiful plastic skin was starting to become dangerously soft from the heat.

"Oh no! It looks like I don't have the liberty of waiting for Ken to rescue me. I need to do something fast."

But what could she do? Although Barbie had never been as known for her towering intellect as for her impressive curves, she tried to reason it out.

"If this abnormal heat was caused by my breaking that mirror and bringing on this bad luck, I need to counteract it by doing something that will bring on some good luck! If I could get to the pink stables without melting, maybe I could get a horseshoe and that would bring me good luck." But she knew she would never make it without melting into a puddle of plastic, paint & oil.

She thought of looking for a four-leaf clover but realized that the abnormal heat had probably killed all the plant life. No, she had to think of something she had in the house that might work.

That hole in the wall was getting bigger and she started to notice—*Oh, no!*—some dimpling of her perfect skin. Suddenly an idea occurred to her. Barbie sprinted into the kitchen as fast as her shapely plastic legs would carry her. She moved to her pink chest freezer and opened it up pulling out a (pink, of course) frozen turkey she had been saving for Thanksgiving. She placed it on the counter and the heat began to defrost it immediately.

"Now all I need to do is wait until it is sufficiently defrosted. Once that happens I can take out its wishbone and pull on it. I will wish that everything was back to the way it was before I broke that mirror. Then if my house was moved somewhere horrible it will return to its usual location or if this is just as extreme case of global warming, that should cure this global warming thing once and for all!"

As she waited for the turkey to melt, another thought popped unexpectedly into her mind. (She never before had more than one.) She again opened the freezer and pulled out a whole chicken.

"Once this heat thing is fixed, maybe I can use the chicken's wishbone to do something about the problem Ken and I have about those anatomically incorrect parts. Wow! I'm almost as much of a genius as Ken."

An afterword to this story is on page 213.

6

A VERY UNUSUAL DAY

by

Sylvia Stein

Amanda Roarke woke up one morning to the sounds of loud banging outside of her window. She tried to ignore them, but then there was a huge explosion that shook her very small apartment from side to side.

What is going on?

She tried to gather some courage to look at the damage. She noticed the date. It was Friday the 13th and Amanda began to feel sick.

Oh no! Did it really happen?

Sadly, Amanda Roarke was a very superstitious thirty year-old woman. It did not help that she had developed a case of Obsessive Compulsive Disorder which caused her to count every forty-five minutes and wash her hands every thirty minutes without fail.

Although Amanda was afraid of what she heard and felt, she managed to gather the courage to look out the window. To her dismay, it looked like a scene from a science fiction movie.

Amanda screamed!

The temperature was rising to a level that made her wonder if there was such a thing as Global Warming. Amanda believed in it, but she didn't want to add one more thing to her already complicated life.

Oh my! I wonder what the temperature is. My skin feels as if it is slowly burning off my body. What is going to happen? Should I take a shower? Is this just a bad nightmare?

Amanda tried to pretend that this all was one big joke. However, as she looked out her door, she knew something disastrous was really happening.

Is the end here? I haven't accomplished as much as I would have liked.

"I knew this day was going to be trouble," she mumbled.

I am so proud to be an American and free. What if things get worse and the world changes? I don't want to lose my liberty.

As Amanda wondered what she should do, she noticed that the day had became even hotter than normal. But she was soon happily surprised to see someone she knew.

"Leo, is that you?" she asked hesitantly.

"Yes, Amanda!" he smiled.

Leo Sanders was her long-time best friend and the man with whom Amanda hoped to spend the rest of her days. They had both grown up in Anders, Texas, just outside of Austin. She was glad he had come to be with her.

"Oh no, Leo, you are burning up!"

"Don't worry Amanda." He added, "I guess this truly is Global Warming."

"How can you joke at a time like this?" she asked.

"You know you love my jokes," he chuckled.

As they walked through the very hot neighborhood, Amanda suddenly began to feel deeply sad.

"Amanda, what is wrong?" Leo asked.

"Leo, what if today is our last day? ' she cried.

"We don't know that for sure," said a more upbeat Leo.

Leo and Amanda could not help but notice how the entire city of Anders was growing hotter and hotter. It seemed like the temperature was rising by the seconds.

Warnings came over a huge intercom.

"We must evacuate the Anders immediately!" exclaimed Mayor Malloy. "We are preparing for a Natural Disaster!"

"Leo, I have to pack" Amanda said.

"Amanda, we must go now. We don't have time for that," he said.

Amanda began to cry as the reality of having to leave the only home sunk in.

"Please don't cry, Amanda!" exclaimed Leo. He then leaned over and gave her a kiss.

"Amanda, I love you," he said.

"I love you too," she said.

Amanda and Leo walked hand-in-hand and never looked back.

An afterword to this story is on page 214.

7

WEST OF LUCKY

by

Arlene Lagos

He was a suspicious kind of man. Even the way his grey dull eyes narrowed, or the lines at the corner of his mouth turned up when he smiled, seemed suspect. From what I hear, he started a fire in the neighbor's barn once. Another time, someone's entire garden spoiled overnight. He was never caught though. But last night was the final straw. Last night he messed with me.

Walking onto my porch to water the plants, I found a dead sparrow. It didn't just drop there either. You could tell by the way it lay, that it was positioned perfectly on top of the step. Anyone who's anyone knows that sparrows carry the souls of the dead. Was he sending me a message?

Walking down the road, he passed my door, radiating a smirk. What does Mr. West *do* anyway? There's nothing extended past the end of our cul-de-sac but woods, so why did he always go that way?

The nosy woman that I am, I had to follow. I'm plain, very quiet and mostly keep to myself except for the occasional book club meeting. But I wanted to know. I have to know what he's up to, what he's planning. Maybe I could catch him red-handed and put him behind bars for good. I'd be the neighborhood hero!

Slipping on my flats, I adjusted my glasses and headed through the house and out the back door, cause it's bad luck to leave a house through a different door than the one I came into. Tiptoeing down the street, sure not to step on any cracks, I finally set foot onto the narrow, smoothed out dirt path before me. There was an odd chill in the air, which I didn't notice at first, of course. We have been familiar with severe weather changes, but it was actually...cold.

Walking further into the forest, I listened intently to ensure I stay close. Suddenly he stopped, and I hid behind a pine tree, making the sign of the cross to protect me. He must not have seen me, so I crouched really low and peeked out from behind the tree. What I saw caused my jaw to drop and a loud gasp to bellow out of my mouth. Mr. West is...frozen! Suddenly, he turned around, and as our eyes locked, I lost my footing and crashed to the ground.

"Sarah, are you okay?" he asked, picking me up.

Again, I made the sign of the cross with my fingers. "Don't touch me, devil!" I screamed.

"Please don't be afraid. I won't hurt you."

"What...are you?"

"I come from Liburtee, a planet outside your galaxy. I crashed here months ago and have been trying to fix my ship so I can get back home." He pulled back some branches revealing a small spacecraft.

"Whoa!"

"You can't tell anyone. Everyone knows what happens to aliens on your planet."

"Area 54."

"Exactly. I can't be experimented on. I just can't, Sarah." He seemed genuinely terrified. Seeing Mr. West up close, he looked different, gentle.

"I won't tell."

Staring at me in awe, he breathed a sigh of relief. "Thank you."

Unaware of what to do, I began to walk back the way I came, only now in a state of confusion. Suddenly I stopped, as I realize the ground beneath me is frozen solid. From behind me, Mr. West pulled a tree branch out of the ground and placed it over the ice, making a bridge.

"How did you do that?"

"Super-strength is just another one our talents."

Walking across the bridge, I stopped and turned around suddenly. "Why did you come here in the first place?" I asked.

"On my planet, I'm a scientist. My people are trying to cure Earth from global warming."

"Of course!" In a daze, I began to walk over the bridge again, feeling my legs moving in one direction as my thoughts drifted in another.

"Well...goodbye," I said.

"Please don't say that," he shouted.

"What?"

"Don't you know it's bad luck if you say goodbye to a friend on a bridge? It means for certain that..."

"That you'll never see them again," I finished.

Right then, my heart began to beat rapidly as I turned on my heel and ran as fast as I could, right into Mr. West's arms. "Take me with you," I said.

"I thought you'd never ask."

As I looked into his eyes and he into mine, he kissed me gently until we were interrupted by an annoying sound nearby.

Bzzz! Recreation time is over. Please line up for your medication.

"We better hurry. It's bad luck to be last."

An afterword to this story is on page 215.

8

ST. JOHN'S LILY

by

Mike Boggia

After the earthquakes, the landscape appeared alien. Huge gashes slashed the earth, creating canyons through the surrounding forest. The dam on the lake below our home breached. It drained, leaving a swamp and raging river. There were other subtle changes too. Most unnerving to adults, animals could talk. My parents, two younger sisters, and I live in our unscathed stone house, waiting for relief from the heat.

Poppa blamed part of our problems on the unnatural, rapid melting glacier fifty miles north of us. "Global warming," he muttered, "will be the death of humanity."

Mamma hushed him. "Don't say that in front of the children, Zeb."

"Look at the thermometer, Connie. It has been 112° for three months. Today it hit 127°, the hottest day we ever had. Without the river, we'd be dried up like most of the country." He wet a towel, threw it over his head, and collapsed in his easy chair.

My sisters and I retreated to the cool cellar.

Starr lowered the book she was reading. "Today's July 17. I wish we could go to see Grammy and Grandpa."

I yawned. "Why?"

"Grammy said her St. John's Lily will bloom at midnight. Maybe we'd see the devil."

"The first bud to open is gold. It has special powers, and Satan picks it so he can have whatever he wants." I chanted the words Grammy used to describe her favorite flower.

"It's a superstition."

Ruby, the youngest, stared at us, wide eyed. "If Grammy says the devil takes the blossom, it's true. She doesn't lie."

"Forget it." Starr picked up her book. "It's too far to walk to Grammy's since the swamp formed. Besides, Poppa forbids us to go near that bog."

"Bet we can find a way there if Cerbe leads us." I looked at the huge Neapolitan Mastiff, snoring on the far side of the cellar. "Cerbe."

He stretched, passed gas, and rolled his eyes at me. "Whatcha want, Gordy?"

"Can you find a short cut to Grammy's house?"

"I already did."

"Will you take us there, tonight?"

"Your parents will kick my tail, Gordy."

"We'll sneak out after they're asleep." My brain churned. "Starr, Ruby, suppose it's true? If we grab the flower, we can save the world."

Starr raised her eyebrows and smiled. "Why not?"

With Cerbe leading, we set out through the moonlit swampland. Starr carried a bag of garlic, Ruby a bottle of holy water and I shouldered my pellet gun. We were ready to do battle. Ruby asked how I planned to get the flower before the devil could snatch it. I whispered my plan. Cerbe, Starr, and I would jump the devil and hold him off long enough for Ruby to snag the flower. Minutes before midnight, we arrived at Grammy and Grandpa's cottage.

We hid behind the recently repaired garden wall and surveyed the flowerbeds. A bud-studded spike stood high above the lily leaves. The topmost tubular showed cracks as the petals prepared to open.

I glanced at my watch and held up three fingers. The wall, shrouded in deep shadow, provided a springboard to launch into the garden. We climbed on top of the stones and crouched, ready to attack.

"Trespassers! Trespassers!" A low-flying great horned owl screamed, swooping over us. We plunged headlong into Granny's Lady Liberty Roses. The girls screamed. I said naughty words.

Cerbe snarled. "Meddling bird. We belong here."

"Hoooh. Do not. Hoooh."

Lights appeared in the cottage. Grandpa charged out the back door, shotgun in hand. "Identify yourselves."

"Grandpa," Ruby sobbed. He lifted us out of the rose bushes and hurried us indoors. Grammy applied Band-Aids on the scratches while Grandpa poured glasses of water for us. They listened while we explained why we were there, between sips of water. Grandpa pointed to the garden where the bud opened before our eyes.

"See, nothing happened. It is a supersti—" His mouth dropped open with a gasp.

A dark figure materialized beside the St. John's Lily and a hand plucked the flower. He held it above his head, turned and glared at us with glowing red eyes. "Your watch is fast, little boy." Cynical laugher echoed from the black form. "Hell on earth continues for another year."

I blinked and the garden was empty. We sat stunned, and then began talking all at the same time. Next year we would be prepared to beat the master of deception and free the earth from his searing grasp.

An afterword to this story is on page 216.

9

WORLD NET UTOPIA

by
Glenda Reynolds

The year is 2235. It has been one hundred fifty years since the global nuclear war nearly wiped out humanity. Parts of the earth are still uninhabited. Tangled steel structures that were once mega-office buildings still litter large cities of the planet along with thousands of abandoned cars that used to run on fossil fuel. The survivors of planet Earth have come together to form themselves one government. Religious structures, religious gatherings, and any kind of religious displays or symbolisms are prohibited. Worship is done only in each man's home. Jihad does not exist nor is there condemnation preached from behind pulpits. The government, known as World Net, actively promotes positive wellness through all media outlets.

Christa is in a good mood as she drives her battery operated Leaf 200 and hums along with the "Let's Be Cheerful" lingo that plays many times each day, courtesy of World Net. After parking the car, Christa walks to her front door and then places her hand on a computer screen for print recognition.

"Welcome, Christa. Be well." The front door opens for her.

All homes are now built with standard remote control event programming, entertainment, and security features. The inside of every house resembles a glass palace with white smooth surfaces much like a sterile doctor's office. Paint of any kind is deemed toxic and therefore is banned. Homeowners are encouraged to have growing walls of plants to purify the air.

Christa tosses her purse on the hallway table. Her clothes are quickly pulled off and tossed aside as she tries to unwind from a day at the office. Five minutes later, her husband, Rob, arrives home from his job as well.

"How was your day?" Christa asked as Rob tosses his wallet and sunglasses on the dresser.

"You don't even want to know. When is dinner?"

"Don't I even get a kiss?" Rob gives her a swift peck on the lips giving her more mustache than lips.

"Well, the day just seemed to drag on forever for me today. There was an employee who was asked to resign after they had warned her repeatedly about wearing her religious jewelry and displaying her religious greeting cards."

Rob's facial expression is now one of annoyance as he replies, "Back in the day, they use to call it freedom of speech. Or was it freedom of religion? Anyway, look what it did to the world. I really don't want to hear about it. I just want to unwind."

"Sweetie, do you want to sit under the Dome while I start dinner?"

"Whatever. Just shut the door behind you."

The Dome looks like a crown with electrodes that affect certain parts of the brain. It is an invention that World Net first used on criminals. They use it to reprogram the minds of offenders, thus cutting down the prison population to almost nothing. Now it is a required use in every home in the one world regime. It gives the user a sense of peace while it also sterilizes humans from procreating unbeknownst to the average man. The World Food & Drug Administration has deemed the Dome to be safe for general use with little side effects. Children are created in labs for couples whose traits are most valued by World Net.

As Christa leaves the bedroom to start dinner, she glances through the window to see a hooded figure place a package in their mailbox. The mystery person is gone by the time she opens the front door. She retrieves the package from the mailbox. It appears to be a homemade DVD. Lucky for her, she still has an old DVD player, a relic from the days of old technology. Dinner could wait a little longer.

The DVD has in fact been made by an underground resistance group to make people aware of the true nature of World Net. In the video, a spokesperson for the resistance tries to convince the viewer that mankind once lived its own life in the pursuit of happiness without government intervention.

People of the world used to have as many children as they wanted. They even ate foods that they knew were bad for them. They exercised free right...

"I like my life just fine, thank you," Christa sniffs, abhorring the very idea that the government has suppressed her rights.

Christa is so agitated that she turns the DVD player off. She opens the bedroom door to find that Rob has just had a session under the Dome. He has showered and dressed in red silk boxer shorts. The heavy smell of cologne filled the bedroom.

"Well, hello, lovely lady. And how was your day?"

An afterword to this story is on page 217.

10

WHAT? WHEN? WHERE?

by

J. R. O'Neill

I laid there for a good while totally unable to get my bearings. The heat was like nothing I had ever felt before. Sweat oozed from every pore on my body and the bed was soaked. Slowly I looked around the room. Everything seemed to be in place, yet out of place at the same time. *What time is it? It must be late, judging by the glow from the windows.* I started to realize that something was wrong. The windows were glowing a deep red color, not the familiar yellow orange that I was accustomed to. And where was my wife, and why had she shut off the air conditioner? I was starting to get angry and panicky all at once.

I took three deep, lung-searing breaths and swung my legs down to the floor and just as quickly pulled them up again. The floor had felt like it was on fire, stinging the soles of my feet instantly. I began to feel the beginnings of a full-fledged panic attack coming on. I tried the calming techniques that the court-ordered shrink had made me practice. Deep breath in, slowly exhale. Nope, that wasn't going to work. My burning lungs were not capable of holding a deep breath for even a second. I scanned the room looking for what? I didn't know. Still, something had to explain what was going on.

I saw my tennis shoes and rushed over putting them on as fast as I could. Even then, my feet were burned. Walking to the window, my panic began turning to dread. Did I really want to know what was on the other side of the curtain?

I stared out for what seemed like an eternity. Gone were the plush, green lawns that had surrounded my house. Gone was the mighty oak that had stood for so long, giving its shade to my yard. Everything was gone. For as far as I could see there was nothing but red rocky desert.

My shiny Lincoln that should have been parked on the crushed shell driveway was gone. For that matter, the driveway was gone, and so was the street that it attached to. Where was my wife?

I left the room and headed down stairs to the kitchen. She must be there, right?

"Vikki!" I shouted to empty air. There was no response. Water, I needed water. I went over to the fridge, but it wasn't there either, I realized then that the sink was missing too, as were the lights, phone, thermostat, and my wife. The woman I took for granted, the woman I belittled on a daily basis, the woman I made cry, the woman I depended on, that woman was now gone.

With great trepidation, I opened the front door. It was like opening the door to a blast furnace. Nothing could live out there.

"You're having a bad dream. You're having a bad dream. You're…" I kept repeating to myself, trying valiantly to wake up.

Not knowing what else to do, I went over to the couch and lay down. I was so tired that the heat soaked up my energy like a sponge does water. I must have dozed off.

"Welcome home!" an evil looking and grossly disfigured aberration said.

"Where am I?" I asked.

"Where you belong," the thing answered.

"Why have you done this to me?" I shouted.

"You did this to yourself, you self-centered, egotistical jerk. Did you really think you could go through life, treating others as though their needs didn't matter? Did you really think there would be no consequences? No, J.R., you were a fool. You threw the love of a great woman back in her face. You lied, cheated, and stole. Now you pay the price. Again, welcome home, the only home you will ever know for eternity."

"J.R., J.R., wake up!" I heard Vikki's sweet voice breaking through the layers of sleep.

The thing spoke as it faded away. "Smarten up, fool, or this is your fate. Your wife's prayers are all that's saving you now!"

I opened my eyes, to find my wife bending over me. Tears were in her eyes. I realized I was lying in a hospital bed. There were doctors and nurses all around me. Yet my eyes were all for my beautiful wife. I remembered the crash.

I now had the liberty to do things differently. What a fool I had been.

An afterword to this story is on page 218.

11

MIDNIGHT SURPRISE

by

H. M. Schuldt

Mrs. Marla Williams had moved into an old traditional house one hot summer day, along with her husband, Mr. Thomas Williams, and their two teenagers, Titus and Jessie. They had just returned from a family reunion where fierce conversations with Aunt June were uncomfortable. Specifically, Mr. Williams had heard enough about so called *temperatures rising in random air pockets*, so said Aunt June who was a loud-mouth sister of Mrs. Williams.

"Your sister, June, is a nut-case," Mr. Williams said, repeating numerous times on the way home to Aberdeen. Doubt spread across his face as he shook his head. "No such thing as global warming."

* * *

Being somewhat of a private person, Mrs. Williams had no intension of going out of her way to meet the new neighbors. In fact, she hadn't gone out of her way to meet anyone in her last neighborhood over the past fifteen years. She wanted peace and she wanted quiet. The thought of knocking on someone's door in her new neighborhood hadn't even crossed her mind. If a neighbor happened to ring her old doorbell, she quickly dismissed the person as nosy or she assumed they wanted something from her.

"Greedy people. They all want something," Mrs. Williams said. She had grown to become suspicious of normal activity just like her sister June had learned to do, but they often ignored strange behaviors. Mrs. Williams insisted on minding her own business until one day, while she was planting yellow marigolds in her new front yard, a small boy, Liam, about six-years old, rode his bicycle right up to her to tell her about what he had seen in her backyard.

"Did you just say the *moon man* comes down from the sky?" Mrs. Williams asked.

"Yes. And he lands in your backyard. And no one believes me, but it really happens," Liam answered. "It does!"

Mrs. Williams played along long enough and listened until she thought she could tell him what he really saw. She thought his childish game was amusing, but she couldn't let him believe such nonsense. "Your mind must have been playing tricks. It does that, you know. You must have seen the temperature change. You know? Global warming."

"What?" Liam asked confused.

"Global warming," Mrs. Williams answered.

"What's that?" Young Liam frowned and opened wide his brown eyes.

"You know how hot it's been outside? Maybe you saw the temperature change in an air pocket. Never mind." Marla wondered if the previous owner had played a terrible trick on the poor boy.

Liam sneezed.

"Bless you," Marla said.

Liam would talk to anyone who would listen. He made it very clear that the lady who used to live in the Williams' house had been taking care of him each week when his mother went to the grocery store. It gave Mrs. Williams the idea to have her daughter babysit the boy since he seemed rather fond of their house, and Liam's mother needed to go buy some food. Young Liam finally sped toward home on his bicycle when he felt satisfied that he could return on Saturday at seven o'clock in the evening.

* * *

Sixteen year-old Jessie Williams welcomed Liam on Saturday night when he came over. The two of them seemed to hit it off pretty well when Jessie showed him her rock collection. "This one is really a shark tooth. This one is petrified wood."

"Way cool!" Liam said wide-eyed. He sneezed.

"Bless you," Jessie said.

"Why do you say, 'Bless you'?"

"To keep bad spirits away."

Marla and Thomas went out for a couple of hours to have a nice quiet dinner at Juliet's Steakhouse while Titus sat playing video games, chatting with boys around the world.

After the sun went down, Liam begged Jessie to go out into the backyard. He explained how the other lady who used to live there, Mrs. Collins, let him see the moon man. At first Jessie did not understand what he meant. They sat down on comfortable patio furniture and noticed how brilliant the stars looked. It was a clear night. A full moon lit up the backyard just as Liam had seen many times before.

"Did you say the moon man sits in our backyard?" Jessie asked.

"Yes. But not tonight." Liam pointed at the full moon. "He's way up there most of the time."

"How does the moon man come down, Liam?"

"Mrs. Collins said he flies," Liam recalled. "She doesn't know who he is. But I know who he is. He's the moon man! He likes it here because it's private."

"What does he look like?" Jessie asked, playing along.

"He sits in the fountain. He is big and white. And he shines! He's very bright," Liam smiled and described him as if something had really been in the backyard.

The next day Jessie forgot all about Liam's imagination until her mother brought it up at breakfast. Jessie wondered just like her mother, what kind of game Mrs. Collins had been playing with this young boy.

* * *

Two weeks later Jessie woke up in the middle of the night. She tossed and turned for an hour. Finally she sat up. Feeling sleepy, she slipped her teenage feet into her fuzzy slippers and headed for the kitchen. Before she turned on the light, something startled her in the dark.

Jessie gasped. Her heart pounded. "Mother! You scared me to death. What are you doing up?"

"Me?" Mrs. Williams whispered loudly. "I couldn't sleep. What are you doing up?"

"I can't sleep," Jessie whispered.

Something caught their attention. Noticing an unusual light coming from a window facing the backyard, they walked over and peered out. There sitting in the fountain was a bright white light.

"What in the world?" Jessie said amazed.

"You've got to be kidding me."

"What is it? A ghost?" Jessie gasped. "Look at it. It has wings. Oh no, have they been clipped?"

"I don't know," Mrs. Williams said. "He's just sitting there. He's so beautiful! Oh, I know. June told me about it. It must be global warming."

"Mother, come on. That's not global warming."

"Then what is it?"

"It must be…"

They murmured together, "The moon man."

An afterword to this story is on page 219.

12

HOUSE ON THE EDGE OF TIME

by
Gene Hilgreen

The clock on the nightstand flashed six-oh-six. Hey, at least it wasn't six-six-six. My head was spinning and yeah, I had a hangover. I must have woken up six times during the night. The same bad dream played repeatedly—I was running—but from what?

Each time when I awoke from the dream, I was sweating. I could remember the last few seconds of it. I was running through dense woods, and then I saw a house. Through the back window, I could see the back of my father's head. He was sitting by himself at the dining room table. The house was the one I grew up in, but the surrounding looked different and nothing else seemed right.

I woke up. It was the day my life would change forever.

The Sunday afternoon meeting was a formality. I already had a signed contract and would start in two weeks. The owner was a multi-billionaire recluse, he owned fifty-one percent of the company, and his daughter owned the rest. I had never met either one of them. They were both in town and just had to meet me. Could I fly out this weekend for a chat? They would make it worth my while.

I took the job because I needed a break, and Chicago is where I was going to get it. I knew the company, and they swore I would not have to deal with the owner. But last night, something happened.

* * *

"Don't worry," they said, "He just wants to meet the great Dr. Jack Edwards."

Well color me honored. This nut job and his daughter want to meet Dr. Jack D. Edwards.

I called an old friend, Jon, who lived outside of the Windy City and told him about the job.

"Hey Jack," he said. "Why don't you stay at my bachelor pad on Lake Shore Drive?"

"Great, I'll call you when I'm near Mother's Pub."

I remembered an exotic car dealer a few blocks from O'Hare. *Why not show some flash?* So I caught a cab.

"What'll it be, son?" said the salesman. I pulled out my Black American Express and said, "I'll take the Ferrari."

The minute I got on Route 90, I floored it and let the big dog eat. I called Jon when I was a couple of blocks from Mother's Pub. It's not that I didn't want to see him, but I wanted to breathe in a little Chicago, before I heard about baseball all night. The table by the window was open and I grabbed it. Now I could see when Jon arrived.

"Would you like a drink?"

I turned to see a raven-haired waitress in a Mother's tank top and red-hot mini shorts that enhanced every curve on her body.

"I'll have a pint of Heinie."

After a few minutes had passed, I turned to see Meg with my beer. This time I caught her nametag.

"Thanks, Meg."

The napkin she placed under the pint had a phone number, a heart with Meg written in it, and under the heart in bold letters, *I GET OFF AT MIDNIGHT.*

My phone rang. When I answered, Jon said he couldn't make it, but he told me where to find the spare key.

***

When I woke up this morning, I got ready for my meeting and figured I'd leave a little early.

The door blew out of my hand when I opened it, and a bird flew over my head. I turned to look for the bird and saw a photo floating to the rug. It was face down. I picked it up and turned it over. It was a picture of me from about twenty-five years ago—a picture Jon had taken at Wrigley's Field.

I closed the door and started down the steps.

A kid on the sidewalk was yelling. "Liberty! Liberty! Come here, kitty!"

A black cat came running across the front yard, stopped, hunched its back, and gave me a mouth full of teeth. Then it disappeared.

I punched the address into my GPS and drove toward Oak Ridge. A cemetery appeared and seemed to go forever. It wasn't there before. Suddenly I saw goats begin to cross the highway.

"What the...?"

When I came to, I was in a ditch in the middle of a cemetery and my head was bleeding. Goat horns were half-through my windshield. Then I saw a gravedigger walking straight for me and sweat was pouring off of him. Well, sweat was pouring off me, too. What was happening? A bird had flown into my house, my picture fell facedown, I crossed paths with Meg and a goat, and now a gravedigger was coming straight for me. I looked at the car temperature reading:

INSIDE 60
OUTSIDE 120

I stepped out of the car and into the heat. Someone had thrown a switch and sent me to this place. I am not superstitious, but everything that happened today says I should be. Sometimes I explain myself, but I still don't get it. Among the top ten superstitions, the black cat should have been a gimme. And now somebody just served me up a full plate of—I told you so. *What is this place?* It felt like I woke up in an alternate universe. It felt like I was in hell.

I started walking toward the house where I grew up. Ok, where did the house come from? I could barely see the house through the trees. Where did the trees come from? I started running.

Then I saw the back of my father's head through the rear window. So I walked around to the front of the house and knocked.

"Come in Jack," said Meg. "My father and I have been waiting for you."

Then I knew I was dead. I could see the man sitting at the table more clearly. It was never my father—it was Lucifer.

"Welcome home, Jack," he said.

An afterword to this story is on page 220.

13

THE GREEN INVISIBLE MOUNTAIN

by

Mirta Oliva

Edward and Lilly were sitting on a swing in their L-shaped front porch overlooking the most picturesque mountain chain they had ever seen. Alongside Mount Green, the tallest one of the group, ran the sparkling Stony Creek. They considered themselves lucky to own this farm even though they were hours away from relatives and distant from neighbors.

"Nature is beautiful. Isn't it, Lilly? Stay with me a little longer to enjoy this colorful sunset before the sun hides away. After dinner, we can watch DVD movies."

"Of course, honey. I love to cozy up with you in front of this spectacular view."

The couple had been outside for a while when Edward shouted as he glanced at the distance. "Lilly, look at the mountains! Do you see an unusual halo way above? It looks...magnificently strange."

"Yes Ed. Look at the glow. Maybe we should get closer to Mount Green to see what's going on."

"Soon it will be dark. Let's wait until the morning. At dawn we can pick the sweetest berries for breakfast while we satisfy our curiosity."

"You are right. It's getting late. I'll go inside now to finish dinner."

"And I'll be feeding the animals," Edward replied.

Even though the couple missed having children, they were able to enjoy the life of their dreams in their little farm. Their two beagles, cows, horses, chickens, and other pets were like the children they could not have. Electricity they had but enjoying telephone service was three months away. They fished at the creek, bartered locally, and sold eggs and veggies to the town market.

The next morning, the couple got up early to go berry picking and to get close to the mountain.

"Sweetheart, I'll be waiting for you outside. Please meet me at the barn."

When Edward opened the door, a cold draft pushed him back inside the house. "Lilly, you have to see this! It is snowing in the middle of this July heat! Lilly, get here quick! Global warming has reduced the mountains to a huge expanse of snow."

"You must be kidding me, right?" answered Lilly. When she reached the door, she quickly replied. "No, you were not joking, but global warming does not make mountains vanish into thin air. And the electric plant is not working, either."

Edward decided not to go outside, not until they had time to digest this odd situation. He was becoming suspicious. Something very strange was happening and he did not know what to do about it. Visibly disturbed, he put his arm around Lilly, taking her slowly to the side window.

"What the dickens? Are we out of our minds?"

From the window they could see the mountain, the green pasture, and no snow. They could hear the trickling sound of Stony Creek's unstoppable cascades.

"Lilly, we saw devastation and snow...and now this! While I stay here at the window, you go to the door for another look."

"Oh no, not again!" shouted Lilly as she uncovered the door's glass panel. "There is snow everywhere, no mountains, and the creek is frozen."

Concerned about their pets, Edward told his wife, "Honey, I must go to the barn to protect the animals from this...inexplicable climate change."

"All right, Ed, but walk carefully. You don't know what's underneath all that snow."

Edward gave his wife a big kiss and walked slowly toward the barn. He was carrying blankets and a walkie-talkie to stay in touch with Lilly if he encountered a problem. Upon entering the building, Edward noticed the animals were gone, including all the chickens. He scattered the blankets on the floor just in case they returned. He painfully told Lilly on the radio what he saw before rushing back to the house.

"I wonder if we should go toward the mountain to see what has happened."

"No, Ed, we should stay inside. We have enough to eat for at least a week, so I'll fix a nice breakfast. We'll have to skip the berries, though."

"I agree. We have been spared from whatever is going on outside. So far, so good. Let's stay at home with the dogs and play games. That's all."

When it got dark, they noticed a splendid glow coming from the window.

"Look, Lilly, there is a huge round object hovering over the snow, almost touching ground where Mount Green was. Look at those colorful beams, pointing in every direction. Oh no! The lights are moving...toward us!"

"Ed, I am very scared!" A crying Lilly continued, "What is going to happen to us?"

"Honey, don't cry. We should keep praying that this whole episode goes away. Let's leave a note on the table, detailing everything in case something happens to us. Then we'll go to bed, hoping for a better tomorrow."

After awakening from what seemed like a long-lasting sleep with horrible nightmares, they rushed to the window. The mountains were there and the animals were outside grazing on the green pasture. However, they still needed to inspect the view behind the front door. Praying for a miracle, they looked outside where they could observe the usual breathtaking mountain-view. As they turned around, they saw the two beagles guarding a basket on the sofa. Inside, there was a lovely baby dressed in a blue gown.

Edward picked up the baby, handing him to his wife while giving both a kiss.

Lilly was quick to announce, "Angel, we'll call him, Angel. A little bundle of love has descended to bring special joy to our home!"

Suddenly, they rushed to the table to see if their "distress message" was still there. And it was! But much to their surprise, it read:

Congratulations! We enjoyed your nine-month stay at the UFO.
- The Aliens.

An afterword to this story is on page 221.

DANGEROUS DAYS

CHAPTER TWO
DANGEROUS DAYS

14

SACK

by

Alli Vaughan

How long had she been here?

The woman continued to stir the pot of food from her sweltering kitchen as she called out to the children in the hallway.

"Salt the back door, sugar the front, remember?" The heat wrapped thick arms around her throat and seemed to steal pieces of her soul away into the scorching furnace of her cramped house.

Three little pairs of legs ran giggling by her. Each wanted to be the first to lay the snow powder lines down across the blue rose tiles. Effie, Adam, and Mona, the youngest.

"Effie," she called, wiping sweat with a golden dishtowel. "Effie, did you hear what I said?"

"Yes," the girl stopped impatiently, eyeing the other children. "It's always the same every night."

"It's important, child. That magic's the only thing keeping the sack man away. He'll take all three of you away in his nasty sack if we should forget even one night."

Effie grinned, eyes dark and evil. "Nothing can keep the sack man away, Jenna. You know that."

Fear and confusion wrapped the woman's face. "What...what did you say, child?" She hadn't been called Jenna since she was young, so long ago. She blinked and looked again, but Effie smiled sweetly.

"I said, *all right*," Effie replied.

Taking a large breath, the woman gripped the counter as the child ran off with the others. "It must be the heat," she whispered under her breath.

It had been hot and awful as long as she could remember. Heat could drive someone to madness, her mama always said. She busied herself in the kitchen and tried to shake away the terrible hallucination and the emptiness of the child's eyes.

"Dinner's ready," she called as everyone ran into the room.

"What we having?" asked Adam, the middle child.

"Maybe we'll feast on her arms and the legs," the youngest, Mona, cooed softly. The child grinned up at the woman's shocked eyes, and Jenna swore she saw sharp fangs in her smile.

Startled, she dropped the ladle of stew clumsily, her slight hands shaking. "Soup, like we always have. Set the table."

Adam laid out the bowls and Mona unfurled the napkins.

The eldest tapped her fingers on the wooden table as Jenna finished filling their bowls. "Don't you ever get tired of this ruse, Jenna? You know we're simply going to eat you."

The woman's eye flew open in surprise. "What are you talking about?"

"Don't bother. The madness has taken her, Effie," Adam said. "She doesn't even know where she is."

"You do know where you are, don't you?" Mona asked sweetly tugging at her sleeve. The woman looked down at her arm, realizing that her clothing was very tattered and needed to be repaired. She would need to sew her clothes tonight.

"Did you hear what she asked?" Effie asked icily.

"I'm in my house." Her reply was so low the children had to strain forward to hear her and when they did, they erupted into a fit of laughter.

The woman's face reddened, but she didn't know why.

"Of course, this isn't a house," Adam blurted between laughs.

"This is the sack man's sack," Mona said, toying with her spoon. "He took you when humans burned the world with poisons and refuse."

Madness lifted a moment, and a flash of memory crossed Jenna's mind. The sack man had come and she remembered his yellow glowing eyes. But that had been a dream.

"It's coming back to her," Effie said, licking her lips.

"Oh goody, we can start the game again." Mona giggled.

"I'll make her cry first," Adam challenged.

"I'll make her collapse and nibble her bones," Mona replied.

A whimper left the woman's mouth and she covered her ears and pinched her eyes closed.

Pain, she remembered pain and torment. Her madness dissolved, she stooped naked and exposed, a soft and weak human among demons. But without the madness as a shield, the memories slammed into her like a wave.

The forests had burned and the sea had boiled red. Even the evil, the shades of their world, even the sack man himself, had condemned the abuse inflicted by the human race. And she had been trapped in this sack. All children of the world had been and the adults had been consumed in the darkness.

So, this was the legacy of punishment her parents had left for her—a scorched planet and a sack man's wrath.

But these were not her mistakes and she would pay for them no more.

Jenna stood resolutely. The demons stepped back, surprised by her confidence.

"Time to leave," the woman announced, balling her fists.

"You can't escape the sack." Their reply came as one voice, guttural and deep. "You'll all stay in my sack for what you've done."

"I will liberate all of the children you've trapped!" Jenna shouted.

"How can you?"

"I don't know, but I'll never stop trying." Tears of desperation filled her eyes.

"And what would you do once you freed yourselves? Ruin the world again? Even fear and darkness cannot live in a world ripped open. Even I hang on the balance of existence."

"We'll make better choices..." she trailed off. "Give us a chance. Let the world return. For good and evil alike."

No reply came and Jenna shivered, afraid she'd angered the sack man. A vibration shook the floor beneath her and the demon children faded into mist. The walls of the house faded as well, and Jenna saw the sack for the first time, shrouded in darkness.

Gentle light trickled through the roof, a crack, no an opening!

The sack opened and Jenna pushed her way out, through the sticky underbelly of darkness and saw the brightest light. Following behind her, hundreds of children came to the new world and stood around her, rubbing their eyes.

Jenna hoped, as she held a blade of orange grass between her fingers, that they would make better choices.

Or else the sack man would return.

An afterword to this story is on page 222.

15

THE SACRIFICE

by

Lynette White

High Priestess Faye Monro stood on the steps of her humble hut and stared at the cloudless sky. After forty-five days of blistering heat the crops were drying up. She could not understand why Hessus, the goddess of life itself, was punishing them like this. Her hours of prayer to the Most Holy Mother in their behalf were answered with dreams she did not understand. The sound of approaching footsteps snapped her out of her reverie. Anglica was coming toward her with her daughter Liberty, born just six days earlier.

The priestess stepped down to join her. "Anglica, why are you out of your birthing bed? Is something wrong with the baby?"

With tears rolling down her cheeks, Anglica cradled the infant closer. "No, Sister. I must speak to you in private." The young mother was trembling from head to foot.

Faye wrapped an arm around Anglica's shoulder. "Yes, of course."

Faye steered Anglica inside to a chair, then settled into a chair next to her. "What is it, Anglica?"

"I am troubled, Sister Faye," she started and looked down at the floor.

"About?" Faye pressed.

Several heartbeats passed before Anglica looked up and answered. "I have had very troubling dreams, Sister, since just before Liberty's birth. Dreams about an altar, Liberty, and a woman holding a dagger with blue lightning dancing upon its blade."

"The woman told me I must sacrifice one to save many," she sobbed.

Faye gasped. "I have had the same dream."

The poor mother found little comfort in this. "Why does this woman want to kill Liberty?"

Faye sat back in her chair and pondered this for a moment. Now she understood the dreams. Liberty was a sacred child. The *setting apart* ritual happened so rarely most of the goddess's followers considered it a superstition. In the twenty-eight years Faye had served as a priestess, even she had never witnessed it. A movement out of the corner of her eye caught Faye's attention. The portal had opened and Sacred Mother Otea beckoned her. Faye stood up.

"Anglica, do you trust me and the Most Holy Mother?"

The mother was frozen to her chair. It took her several moments to answer. "Yes," she squeaked.

Faye moved to the open portal. "Then come with me."

Anglica finally moved and sucked in her breath as Faye took her hand and pulled them through the portal. Anglica looked around in a panic as they emerged in a distant land. The only thing familiar to her was the hut, simply because it looked just like Faye's.

An elderly woman dressed in a simple white cotton dress opened her arms in greeting. "Faye, Anglica, come inside quickly as we must not keep the Most Holy Mother waiting."

Otea tried to rush them inside, but Anglica paused.

"Trust me," Faye whispered.

Anglica nodded dumbly and moved inside. Standing beside the altar in the back of the hut was the woman from their dreams, right down to her face concealed by the hood of her cloak.

"Anglica, my child, you have come." The woman spoke in a gentle voice. "It pleases me to see the faith in your heart."

"I do not understand?" Anglica questioned.

"Liberty is a sacred child, Anglica. Preordained to serve as High Priestess or perhaps as Sacred Mother. The Most Holy Mother is here to set Liberty apart," Otea explained.

"Please place the child upon the altar," the woman instructed.

Before she could fully comprehend what was happening, Anglica obeyed. The woman reached into her cloak and drew out the athame. All eyes were drawn to the deep blue lightning flashing on the blade. The woman adjusted the athame so it was straight above Liberty's right shoulder. Within a few heartbeats the blade touched the child's skin, lightning crackled, the baby cried, and Anglica screamed.

The athame returned to the woman's cloak, and Faye's eyes locked onto the fresh lightning bolt scar on baby Liberty's shoulder.

"Take your sacred child home, Anglica. Someone will come for her in eight years on the date of her birth. Because of your sacrifice you will be blessed all of your days," the woman instructed and pulled back her hood.

Faye gasped as she looked into the gentle face of a goddess. It was but an instant before Hessus vanished. Anglica dropped to her knees, scooped up her infant daughter, and began to weep uncontrollably. Faye turned toward the open portal. Raindrops were spotting the windows of her hut.

"The sacrifice of one will save many," Faye whispered.

An afterword to this story is on page 223.

16

THE ENCHANTRESS

by

Connie Flanagan

Meri came to the village when I was 12, the summer I was betrothed to Moses. Everyone was excited, because people so rarely moved between villages due to the ongoing wars among them. Each successive growing season was hotter and more arid, so food was scarce, and every village fought with the others for survival. Meri was approved by the Elders since she was a merchant of childbearing years, and the women of the village talked about nothing else in the days before she arrived. The only house available to her was the decrepit two-story across the street from ours, so I was able to observe her closely.

Meri was as short as a nine-year-old child, with dry white hair and pallid skin that didn't even flush in the sweltering heat. Her eyes were reddish, like those of our white rabbits. I'd never seen anyone like her. She was skeletal, her gaunt face making her peculiar eyes protuberant. I wondered from what harsh village she had come and why she'd been allowed to leave.

That first day she kept to herself across the street in the house that was really too large for one person. The Devlins had previously lived there before all six of them were eventually killed in a series of wars against neighbouring villages.

That night when I went out to relieve myself, I spied candlelight flickering around the edges of the house's drawn blinds. What was she doing in there while all decent folk were abed? I shivered with trepidation and scurried back to my straw pallet.

The following day was a scorcher, so I had to run out early to bring brackish water to the men in the fields. When I returned, Meri had set up shop. On a battered oak table in front of her house were glass jars, inside of which were what looked like large spherical rubies. The sun shone through them, creating colourful shadows resembling those cast by the church windows. Already she was encircled by all of the boys too young to work in the fields. Noah, my younger brother, was with them.

My mother spat on the ground in greeting. "Nothing but coloured sugar!" she said in disgust. The women had been hoping for a seamstress or a weaver.

I watched Meri from the doorway. None of the boys had coins, but she just laughed, flashing badly decayed teeth, and gave them the sweets anyway.

Their mothers gave Meri scathing looks, asking each other what kind of merchant gave her wares for free and what she would eventually demand in exchange.

When my father and the other men, including my two older brothers and my betrothed, came home for the midday meal, the women poured out their vitriol, demanding that the men do something about Meri.

"Lisbeth," my father said sadly, "the boys will be working in the fields or going to war soon enough. Let them have some pleasure while they're young."

The other husbands said pretty much the same, and soon Moses, my older brothers, and their friends were pushing the younger ones aside to sample Meri's treats. Blood-red saliva ran in slow rivulets down their chins. I shuddered, reminded of slaughtered livestock and past wars.

Like the other women and girls of the village, I kept my distance from Meri. Just looking at her made the fine hairs on my arms and the back of my neck prickle. Many of the women crossed themselves or made the sign of the horns to ward off the evil eye as they watched their sons crowd around her.

While my father and the other married men readied themselves to return to the fields, the single men continued to throng Meri. Again the women expressed their consternation, but their husbands said that another war between the villages was imminent, so to let the young men enjoy this special treat. Besides, today was really too hot for them to work.

My mother thought my father was either a fool to underestimate Meri's awful influence, or he was as besotted as his imprudent sons were by this vile woman. Although she wouldn't speak against him, my mother's eyes were dark, and her mouth was grim.

Later that afternoon as I watched from my shaded doorway, Meri scooped up a jar of sweets and declared that she was going for a walk. The boys and young men followed her as though enchanted.

"Moses," I hissed at my betrothed from the shadows. He reluctantly turned to face me.

"Where are you going?" I demanded.

An absurd grin on his face, he shrugged. "After the others," he replied with a wave of his arm before running to catch up.

Although the shimmering heat made me lightheaded and nauseated, I surreptitiously followed Moses and the others. Meri sang and sashayed as they all shambled after her with glazed eyes, pushing each other to be closest to her. Down the dusty main street they snaked, a tattered parade oblivious to the searing sun.

When they exited the village, my heart skipped a beat. It was risky to leave the safety of the village because women my age were often stolen to bear children for other villages. Despite my misgivings, I continued tailing them.

They veered off the road and crossed a field full of thistles and rocks. To my horror, I suddenly realised where Meri was leading them. I tried to scream, but my throat closed on the thick air. With a sprightly skip and a wry smile, Meri turned at the edge of the cliff to gaze at the boys.

"Come along," she crooned, "'ere war and famine seize you! This is the only path to true liberty!" With a flourish, she scattered the sugary jewels over the cliff, and with them went the boys and young men of my village. Before jumping after them, Meri caught my eye and winked.

An afterword to this story is on page 224.

17

FOUR SHADOWING

by

Neil Carroll Ellison

My mother fell to the ground in anguish as I stepped from the car. I looked down. Between the twin shadows cast by my leg, I saw that my shoe was covering the tiniest of fissures in the driveway.

She clutched the small of her back. "I think it's broken. I can't feel my legs."

"Ma, it'll be OK. It was a really tiny crack, maybe a five-minute crack. I'll be more careful next time."

"You'd better be! Remember the last time you weren't careful and stuck your foot in that pothole? I was in the hospital for a month!" She had to remind me.

Stepping on a crack won't always break your mama's back, but the severity and duration of her injury are directly related to the size of the crevice. Step on a small one, she hurts for a few moments. Step on a big one, she's in the ICU.

I carefully tiptoed from the car into the brown grass of her yard. Our two suns had been wreaking havoc on anything green for the past ten years or more. They'd been pretty hard on people too.

"How long ya gonna leave me out here in this heat, Jimmy? Huh?"

"Ma, you know I can't move you if your back is broken. I'm sorry. It'll only be 5 minutes, honest. Lemme get you a couple of umbrellas. That'll keep the suns off ya until you can stand up."

I ran into the house before she could protest. It was the house I grew up in. I still call it home even though I moved out two decades ago. It's a modest split-level ranch. My parents put a lot of work into the place when they bought it. The décor that had not been destroyed by the previous owners was woefully stuck in the 1960s. Other than the dark wood paneling in the bedrooms and discarded avocado vinyl chairs, the worst feature of the place was the floating staircase highlighted by a mural of blue, yellow, and orange rectangles that looked like it had been vomited by Mondrian.

The family who had previously owned it had six kids, a dog, and a matronly maid. I think the father was an architect. They were briefly famous as a template for the All-American nuclear family, but they trashed the place when a scandal forced them back to their base elements—consisting of one parent and three children of the same sex. No one knows what happened to the maid.

I quickly found the umbrellas in a stand just inside the door. Not all conventions from the 60s were useless. By the time I got back to the front yard, Mom had made it to her knees. Blades of dry, brown grass covered her blouse. Dust clouds rose from where her knees pressed into the yard. As I approached her from behind, my dual shadows encircled her from the left and right like first responders coming to her aid.

"Gimme that," she said, snapping the umbrellas from my hands. "It's too hot out here. Hotter than yesterday. It wasn't like this in May when I was a kid, I tell ya. May was springtime. Flowers, rain, trees buddin'. Now it's just heat and more heat."

"I know, Ma. We're gonna hav'ta stay inside on the fourth again this year. Remember last year when it was so hot that the fireworks blew up all by themselves? They're sayin' July's gonna be even hotter this year."

"Celebratin' liberty by bein' a prisoner in my own home ain't bein' free, I tell ya. Air conditionin' or not."

"I know, Ma," I said rolling my eyes. I'd heard the same rant for the past fifteen or so years. Ever since the news people started talkin' about global warming. Now that was all she could talk about. It used to be the high price of gas that her world centered on, now it's the heat of the day. Granted, it has been getting hotter annually for the past fifteen years, so maybe she isn't so crazy.

The first five years weren't bad. The extra heat was barely noticeable, actually rather pleasant. Summers were a few degrees warmer. That was just another excuse to go to the beach or build a pool. The home improvement portion of the economy boomed. The past 10 years though, they were BAD. As a species we felt like lobsters in a collective pot being brought to a boil slowly, so we wouldn't notice.

But the extra heat isn't without its perks. Cooking stones had become standard patio equipment, a nice dark flat stone that absorbs the suns' rays for a perfect cooking surface. No electricity or gas was required. It gave no extra heat in the house like the oven. Although, what money we save on utilities for cooking, we more than spend in cooling.

"C'mon, Ma, let's go inside. I'll cook you a nice patio steak. Happy Mother's Day."

I helped my mother to her feet. She hugged me and said, "Thank you." I'm not sure if it was for offering to cook or for getting her out of the suns. We walked inside and left our four shadows on the front step.

An afterword to this story is on page 225.

18

ALL IN A DAY'S WORK

by
D C Mills

I wake up soaked in sweat. The light filtering in speaks of morning, though the alarm clock by my bed insists that it is only 4:18 a.m. Nothing unusual in that. This is summer, the white nights when the sun sets for only a few hours, and it never gets really dark. I struggle out of the damp, clinging sheet and push the window further open, hoping for a cool dawn breeze. But no, the air is as still and arid as it has been for several weeks now, and even the birds, normally so annoyingly bright and cheerful at this hour, seem mugged.

I decide to get in my morning run before the temperature rises any higher, so I get into the smallest possible running gear that is still decent, drink as much water as I can stomach, and set out.

I run every day. In my line of work, running is not a fashionable leisure activity, but a survival skill. I would rather not begin to count the number of times I have been saved by my ability to run away from someone or something nasty that wanted to do unspeakable things to me. And I am not being Victorian here. I really do mean unspeakable.

Quite a few other runners are out and about this early, working around the altered weather conditions.

We are all trying to adapt—Vikings getting accustomed to a tropical life—well, not tropical, exactly. The last few winters have been exceptionally cold, with frost and masses of snow lasting well into April. Then a sudden, short spring sets in, and summer right on its heel. The meteorologists have had to come up with a new definition of "heat wave." The old one consisting of three days in a row over 28 degrees Celsius has become a joke. Now we have temperatures well into the thirties for weeks on end, months even. And droughts to rival the Australian outback.

Today is *The Day*, Friday the 13th of July, when everything has to be resolved or the world will go to hell in a handbasket.

It is going to be a long day.

When I return, a black cat is sitting on the garden fence glaring at me. "Hello, Shadow," I say. No reply. He is understandably put out by my blatant selfishness in not feeding him before going out. I point out that he wasn't around, but he refuses to speak to me until I have given him a whole tin of tuna.

Yes, I know I'm a cliché—a witch with a talking black cat. So sue me.

After a cool shower and a big mug of coffee, I set about gathering the appropriate spells and ingredients for today's work. Shadow, with the sense of occasion so peculiar to cats, paws at my knitting, but gives it up when I ignore him. I cannot be bothered about losing a woollen sock right now. The circle at the bottom of my garden needs to be fortified, so that's where I'll begin.

A circle of smallish granite menhirs sits unobtrusively inside a copse of oak trees, planted in concentric circles. Oaks are the strongest and most powerful of trees, drawing ancient powers from the soil and storing them in their massive boles. It is no coincidence that the Druids of Gaul and Britannia revered the oak above all other trees.

And I am going to need those powers to bind and hold the force that is causing this havoc to our climate. For I know now what it is—a Khaos being, an incorporeal will using its temporary liberty only to disrupt and destroy—not from any active malevolence or ill will towards mankind, mind you, just for the kicks.

Wearing nothing but a loose-flowing silk robe—even that feels like a fur coat today—I trace the inner circumference of the menhirs with salt, leaving a small opening. Next, I trace the outer circumference in the same manner, weaving binding spells into the lines. I place a silver bowl in the centre of the multiple circles and with my silver athame cut open my left palm. I let my blood drip into the bowl and then wrap a cloth around my hand. No drop must be allowed to fall on the ground inside or outside of the circle. I step out carefully, closing first the inner and then the outer salt circles with locking spells.

Only blood will summon the Khaos creature. Salt and stone and oak will hold it.

I hope.

When I begin the summoning chant, smoke rises from the bowl of blood—wispy at first, but gradually, it grows into a thick, spiralling column, reeking darkly of gore and rot. The Khaos being resists the summoning, fights against the binding. My muscles ache. My joints feel like they are on fire. Still, I chant. The spell must not be broken before the binding is complete.

After what feels like days, the howling of the smoke subsides, and the column itself dwindles down to a puddle inside the bowl. I feel the grip on me relax, and I have to work not to sink into a puddle myself.

I tremble and then realise that the tremor is in the ground beneath me. The granite menhirs are shaken, begin to sway and then topple inwards, crumbling. All around me, the massive oaks are swaying and groaning. I manage to pick myself up and run, away from the circle, before the innermost ring of oaks creaking and cracking fall on top of the stone debris.

When the rumbling stops, a dust cloud hovers over a jumbled pile of stone and wood, slowly settling in the still, dry midday air.

Exhausted, I have another cool shower and a nap.

I wake up covered in goose bumps. A cool afternoon breeze carries the scent of rain into my room.

An afterword to this story is on page 227.

19

IN THE COOLER

by
David Russell

Tom, the proprietor and owner along with his wife, Terri, of Tom's Market in the mid-Atlantic town of White Oak, Maryland, had heard the weather forecast from WASH FM. Early that July morning much was the same as previous days—hot, hazy, humid, mid 90s, and a 20-30% chance of rain. The air-conditioner at his convenience market was a few years old but reliable. It kept the interior of the store cool and comfortable.

"Just place those cases in the cooler," Terri advised the delivery man who dropped off bottled waters, various brands of soda, and energy drinks each week to the store.

He had the cooler re-stocked and a check in hand from the owners within a half hour of his arrival. The store hours were from 7 AM to 7 PM, seven days a week, and most store items were delivered during the first hour of business. The couple hired part-time help so they could occasionally get away from the store themselves.

This particular day was Tuesday and a couple hours after the store closed, something unexpected began to occur that was caught on the security camera. The cooler seemed as if it were making stretching, yawning, somewhat canorous sounds.

There were slight shuffling sounds heard from inside the cooler.

"Hey, how long do you think we will be in here?" an energy drink inquired.

Pepsi soon replied, "I don't mind it in here. Feels pretty cool compared to the factory and delivery truck."

Verners added, "Yeah, those metal crates with little side padding can be quite unnerving."

Coke recalled, "My parents used to talk about how glass bottles were jangled and clunked about as they made their journeys from factory to across town or across country. Some had neuroses by journey's end from the stress induced."

Canada Dry, the only international in the group added, "I, too, like it in here. Besides, I like knowing that providing someone refreshment—via my coolness and flavor—will be well received and I might even cure someone's gastric reflux. I am glad we come with twist-tops. Sure beats being poked and prodded with an opener."

Conversation continued ranging from the legacy the bottles wanted to leave to business, to recalling the history of the bottled beverage and its impact on life globally.

Over the next few days, the number of bottles gradually dwindled and the cooler became roomier. By Saturday evening, they would all likely be dispersed, fulfilling their respective mission and purpose in life.

At noontime Saturday, a couple of Verners, energy drinks, and bottled waters remained. As was customary, earlier morning hours would see other food items take center stage. They included the sausage sandwich, assorted sweet rolls from the nearby bakery, and even Terri's hard-boiled eggs sprinkled with garlic, canola and a hint of pepper to taste.

Just shortly after noontime Saturday, three giggling, smiling, snickering, casually-dressed US Marines entered the market. They were in the middle of a 96 lingo for long weekend. They had stopped to pick up some chips and drinks for a picnic they were going to have with some coed Marines who, like them, were trained at Paris Island in South Carolina.

As they approached the cooler, something unique began to occur. The bottles with labels facing the front began to sing in unison:

We are here for you,
Take us if you care.
We are bottled for you,
With pleasure to share, here, always,
And only for you.

Tom inquired somewhat firmly, "Hey, what the dickens is going on over there?"

One of the group replied, "A phenomenon, to be sure, not like the MLB 2013 All Star game, mister."

The others laughed.

Moments later, Tom walked over to the cooler and again, the bottles sang their chorus. He made a quick decision. "Men, you can have these 6 drinks for a dollar. It's my token of thanks to you for serving God and this country."

A slightly taller broad-shouldered Marine answered, "Thanks, mister. The girls will be impressed with our ability to stage a picnic."

The bottles were put in a cardboard pack, bagged, and happy to be together, embarking on their mission, and sharing their purpose in life—to refresh and renew. As they left the store, the bottles thanked to Tom and Terri for caring for them over the past week.

By mid-week word had spread of the occurrence at Tom's market. The store security camera had recorded the entire event including the bottle song. The song became a major hit on MySpace and YouTube. It was even featured on the morning show on Q107.3 from Washington radio. Additionally, CNN News Fox News and the Food Network reported the Tom's Market event a few times during their respective broadcast days for a couple of days. Six months later, during the State of the Union Address, the U.S. President nationally recognized Tom, Terri, and their market for contributing to commerce and the American way of life.

Over the next few years, the market enjoyed a steady stream of business year-round by those going to leisure spots or coming home, having been renewed and revitalized from time well-spent.

An afterword to this story is on page 228.

20

SUMMER MAGIC

by

Rebecca Lacy

The summer when I was six years old was filled with magic. There's simply no other word that can describe those long, sultry days spent with my mother, lying on a blanket under a big shade tree in our front yard. We spent hours watching the clouds pass overhead, making up stories about where they had come from and where they were headed. Once she pointed to a particular cloud and told me the most wonderful story about it.

"Look closely, Mia. Do you see an animal when you look at that cloud?" she asked me.

I nodded, and she said, "It might look like a regular cloud, but it is a really lovely llama named Suzie. She was born on a farm where she used to herd sheep. She had lots of friends and was very happy then."

"Why is she a cloud now instead of a llama?" I asked with wide-eyed wonder.

"Gladys is responsible for that," she answered with the same note of disappointment in her voice that she used when I misbehaved.

"Who's Gladys?"

"Gladys," explained my mom "is a naughty little mouse."

"A mouse?" I couldn't believe my ears. Dad always complained about how terrible mice were when they got into our corn. I didn't see how a mouse could turn a llama into a cloud, and I told her as much.

"Well, Gladys isn't just any old mouse. She's a witch."

"A witch?" I asked in horror. "Can she turn me into a cloud?"

"No, dear, she can't. She can only practice her witchcraft on animals."

"Why is she so mean?" I asked, big tears threatening to roll down my cheeks.

"Well, you see, Gladys is terribly lonely, so she travels the earth in search of friends. When that happens, Gladys becomes sad and wants to make the other animals sorry that they weren't nicer to her. That's when she turns them into clouds."

Just then Suzie seemed to nod her head as though confirming that the story was true, and then she trotted off toward the horizon.

That summer, my mother introduced me to a veritable zoo of cloud animals. She knew each of their life stories and names. Sometimes they would linger for a while, doing tricks to entertain us or showering us with playful rain. Most people think that clouds only pass by once, but that isn't so. Those that are really enchanted animals like to stop by every few days to say hello.

One day we were having a nice chat with a baby elephant named Mali, who liked to squirt rain at us from his trunk. I asked my mom if the clouds could ever become real animals again. She looked thoughtful for a few seconds before answering. "Yes, they can, but only if Gladys removes the spell that she has placed on them. However, there is a cost for that to happen."

"A cost?" I asked.

"Yes. You see, the only way that Gladys will free the animals is to make a new friend who she knows will never leave her—someone who would love her even when she is naughty."

"You mean like you love me even when I'm naughty?" I asked.

"Yes," she said, "but someone must love her without conditions."

I didn't quite understand what that meant, but it made me feel good to know that there was hope for my friends.

It was at the close of that magical summer when my mother died. In her final moments she gave my hand a squeeze that reminded me of butterfly wings. She whispered, "Give my best to Suzie."

There followed an unearthly quiet as though every living thing had frozen. The only sound that I could hear was the tick of the clock on the mantle in the next room. No one breathed. No one spoke.

Suddenly, it was as though all the clouds that we used to tell stories about were mourning my mother's passing. The sky turned black, and a great rolling thunder shook the house in a long anguished sob, followed by torrential rain.

That night, my sleep was filled with dreams of my mother telling me not to worry about her. Surrounding her were some of our favorite cloud friends coming up to nuzzle her, making her laugh. Oddly, they had all assumed their earthly animal shape.

I woke the next morning to running feet and shouts. Even though I was very young, I recognized the sound of anxiety in their grown-up voices, and I worried what it meant. I wanted to see what was happening, so I ran outside in spite of the fact that the adults tried to stop me. I was greeted by the most amazing sight. There were Suzie and Mali and every other cloud that my mother had shown me. They were back in their animal form just as I had seen them in my dream.

I still miss my mother, but I'm happy that she and Gladys are friends. All of the animals who were once clouds are now living on our farm, and I no longer have much time to sit under the shade tree. I guess that doesn't matter since there aren't nearly as many clouds to watch these days. I must say, sometimes I do miss the rain.

An afterword to this story is on page 229.

21

SHADOW CHILDREN

by

Karen Beck

Skin, supple and baby soft, rolled beneath my fingertips. I touched my face, felt the plump apple of cheeks, and allowed my hand to slide from forehead down the bridge of my nose until it found, and encircled, a newly taut neck.

I didn't recognize my hands, but it seemed a small matter. Gone were the mottled age spots and engorged purple veins. These hands—now mine—were white and tender as dove's wings, a delightful duo capable of playing music, of buttering a slice of toast, of wriggling around without pain or strange arthritic clicks.

"Are you satisfied?"

I smiled, more at myself than at the surgeon. I strummed my arms, played my fingers over dimpled knees, admiring the miracle he'd wrought. This body, meant only as a temporary vessel, was a vast improvement over the others I'd inhabited.

"You, Doctor Grafton, will be magnificently rewarded."

"Nonsense," he said. "What we do—all of us—we do for the good of the people."

I stood, took my first tender steps. Spun, affecting a perfect pirouette.

"Careful, my child," he chided, cupping me beneath my arms and legs, returning me to my hospital bed. "These feet, and soon your mind, are not your own."

His voice fell dreamily as I lay still and awaited the injection that carried my mission. "Can you hear me?" he asked, but I couldn't answer.

I was already swimming, drowning in the cerebral pool of a little girl's dreams and wishes...

* * *

"I am home, Mama." I announced myself, as was my custom. Upon hearing my voice, the tumblers in the door lock uncoupled and the front door unlatched. My home, a simulated-thatched roof cottage in the echo-chambers beneath Wales, smelled strongly of burnt coffee and spent flowers. I called out, alarmed to find the vestiges of a private wake in our living room.

Two years ago, I lost my younger brother to The Surface. He'd sleepwalked unprotected, slipping from the safety of the biosphere into the brutal first rays of sunrise. Only recently had my family qualified for underground World Counsel Housing based on my father's research in Thermal Redirection. I sat on the couch surrounded by rotting wreaths and old photo albums. I waited, my thoughts flipping from Ishmael's closed-casket service to what I saw now.

"You must not think..." Papa's voice filtered into the room via intercom. "You must never allow yourself to believe she's alive."

"How can I do anything but think, Samuel?" Mama responded. "She was all we had left."

I ran to the door, arms outstretched, tears falling unchecked. The wake, the flowers…all of it was wonderfully meaningless. "Mama, Papa!" I shouted. "Why did you leave me?"

"May God preserve us," Papa muttered, his legs buckling beneath him. Mama rushed forward, her hands fluttering across my hair and face.

"It is you, little Angelica…isn't it?" Mama drew me close, my father hovering just inside the doorway. I turned to him with outstretched arms, still held in my mother's grasp. Papa knelt, touched my face—and wrenched me from my mother.

"Papa—" I screamed, "you're hurting me!"

"What have you done with her, filthy changeling," he growled. He shook me, a madman with a rag doll. "Where have you taken my Angelica?"

* * *

"You have a choice, little Angelica. Though I admit it isn't a fair one." The doctor muttered.

With his assistance, I struggled from the gurney. My new body, old and gnarled, defied my brain's simplest instruction. I limped toward the window separating me from the nursery, the brightly lit room filled with others exactly like myself: Children forever trapped in worn adult bodies.

"There is no chance?" I asked.

"Hope is fool's gold, little one," he said, shaking his head. "Your father murdered your body, correctly suspecting it sheltered the mind of a spy. Unfortunately, he also destroyed the Revolution's opportunity to accelerate his work."

We stood side by side, watching old children play. A tossed ball fell, bounced and rolled toward us. An attendant, flush with youth, hurried to retrieve it.

"So my fate is to live here..."

"Or die." He shrugged, resolved to abide by my wishes. "I assure you, it will be fast and painless."

My mind was tender, imprisoned in an elderly woman's body. Somewhere beyond these walls, Mama lived and Papa worked. Leaning against the glass for support, I tottered toward the nursery. The door swung open.

I was still young enough to hope.

An afterword to this story is on page 230.

22

THE INVITATION

by
Shelly Heskett Harris

Pearl stood on her front porch and watched the smoke bellow out of Cypress Canyon. The temperature was well over a hundred, and the dry underbrush seemed to welcome the wind-driven flames. In the distance, two planes were dropping water, and fire-fighting crews were working point on the blaze. She judged that the conflagration was charging directly at her, about two hours away. There was only one road out of the canyon. She had waited too long.

She'd lived in this house on this ranch all of her life. "Ranch," she said to herself and snorted. At one time everything she could see from her porch belonged to her family. The endless years of Texas drought had first forced them to run smaller herds, and then it became necessary to sell off land to pay taxes. In the last of her line, only the house and a few acres remained.

A small red insect, dizzy from the smoke-laden air, landed on her arm. "Ladybug, ladybug, fly away home," she recited. "Your house is on fire and your…" The words caught in her throat.

Pearl turned to go inside, but a blur of movement down the hill startled her. A doe and a fawn ran across the pasture with three gnomes in clumsy pursuit.

"That's unusual," she said aloud and looked around the yard to see if any others were about. A small head popped up from behind an agarita bush. Pearl waved hello and gave the all-clear signal that meant she was alone. Two gnomes scurried up the hill and joined her on the porch.

* * *

Pearl could barely remember the first time the little ones had allowed her to see them. It was after Jake died. She had been trying—by herself in the rain—to load the last of the calves for market. The price was dropping every other week. It was imperative they go now. The Briggs boys were off to Liberty College and couldn't help. No one else could help, either. She shivered, remembering her feeling of utter aloneness mixed with helpless defeat.

Then the miracle. She was surrounded by small humanoid creatures, who began to magically load her livestock. Her despair turned to awe and then, as the years passed, to a comfortable relationship bound by mutual respect. In some cases, like one young gnomish couple, genuine affection grew between them.

* * *

"The Old One sent us to check on you," Arzo said with formality to show he was on a mission of importance. He wore the traditional bright pointed cap with a matching vest and a serious expression. "He wants to know, do you want to come with us to the magical world?"

Pearl almost smiled at his discomfort, but was surprised by the invitation. "Is there any fire there? I thought everything in this realm also happens in your world."

"It does, but not as destructively," Esdd said. She, too, was controlling her usual bouncy nature. "We are stewards of the seeds."

"Of course, I should have realized, you're stewards of the seeds." Pearl said. She thought a minute, and her voice caught as she indicated with her hand the only home she had ever known. "This has been my home. But my work is done here. Yes, I will go with you to your world."

An afterword to this story is on page 231.

23

THE FORTUNE COOKIE SURPRISE

by

Lynn Johnston

It was a mysterious magical place according to rumor. Considering how mundane her life had become, Melanie hoped it was true. Working as a librarian had to be the dullest life ever.

I've only read about great adventures—never had any of my own. Life is no fun, unmarried and without children.

Looking about the Chinese restaurant, she decided it too, was a letdown. The magical ambiance she felt when stepping through the door had faded, leaving her with a familiar emptiness. Just before leaving, she snapped her fortune cookie in half, removing the slip of paper before promptly stuffing it in her pocket.

After leaving the restaurant, she hailed a taxi. Melanie gave the driver her address and jumped in. Clearly going the wrong direction, she made a futile attempt to argue with the foreign cab driver who seemed to speak little English. He dropped her off by the curb at the airport.

"I said *Jaffky Street*, not JFK!" she argued, but he took her money and sped away.

Feeling frustrated at the inconvenience, she looked for another taxi, then spotted a man she hadn't seen in months. It was Rafi from the antique shop she frequented. He recognized her at once.

"Hi, Melanie, nice to see you. I'm meeting Maria. She'll be anxious to see you." He invited her to accompany him to the waiting area.

When Maria stepped off the escalator, she was thrilled to find Melanie with her husband. They stood in the lobby catching up while Maria explained about her annual trip home to Italy where she could find the neatest things to sell in her antique shop. Pulling a trinket out of her purse, she placed it in Melanie's hand.

"What do you think of this?"

"It's gorgeous!" Melanie exclaimed. "Where did you find such a unique piece? I bet it's a hundred years old!"

"It's actually about fifty years old. My sister had several of them. She gave one to me," claimed Maria.

"It's exquisite!"

"You like it? It's yours."

"No, I couldn't, Maria. It belonged to your sister."

"Nonsense. I insist." Maria cupped both hands around Melanie's.

Melanie knew from her expression not to argue. Smiling appreciatively, she kissed Maria on the cheek.

Rafi, appearing tired, took Maria's hand and began walking towards baggage claim. Melanie gently placed the trinket in her purse as she waved *good-bye* to her friends. Knowing it would have been both inconvenient and presumptuous of her to ask her friends for a ride home, she headed to the exit to find another taxi.

An airport security woman tugged Melanie's right arm and said, "Ma'am, you need to come with me."

"What? Why?" Melanie questioned in a perplexed tone.

"You were seen concealing an item in your purse. Would you please remove it?"

Complying with the request, Melanie stopped walking, opened her purse, and removed the item. "It's just a little gift my friend gave me."

The officer took it from Melanie to examine it closely. "Like I said, you will need to come with me."

"If you give me a moment, I can call my friend, and we can clear it up."

Unconvinced, the woman kept walking as she led Melanie to an office. "This should only take a few minutes."

Grabbing a clipboard, she told Melanie to take a seat. Melanie's pulse raced, and she couldn't fathom what would happen next. She kept asking herself what could be so special about an antique Italian ring case. After several minutes of questions, the woman ordered, "Wait here. It might be a while."

Feeling exasperated, she pondered over possibilities. *What if this takes hours? What if they arrest me? This could turn into a mess...if I get arrested, I could lose my job.*

Panicking, she gazed about the office and spotted a door. Not knowing where it led, she decided it would be worth a try. She jiggled the handle, and it flew open into a busy hallway. *Perfect.* She darted down the hall as fast as she could and sped into a nearby bathroom.

As she wondered how long she should take refuge there, she washed her face. No sooner had she dried it off, she heard, "Liz! There you are!"

Liz?

A thin blonde wearing a thick glasses and a sweatshirt with the letters *BSC*, tugged on her arm. "Thank God I found you! Our flight will be leaving shortly."

"Our flight? Melanie inquired.

"Yes. Come with me." Walking briskly, the lady led Melanie down a hall. "I am surprised you would have left your boarding pass and passport just sitting there when you left for the restroom. I took the liberty of grabbing them for you."

Melanie peeked at the passport picture and was astonished to see how much she resembled someone named Elizabeth Dalton. She decided that being mistaken for someone else was better than being arrested, so she continued with her facade, trying to keep pace with the fast-walking blonde. When they arrived at a gate, they were greeted by a large group people wearing the same *BSC* sweatshirt. Just as Melanie was boarding the plane, she glanced over her shoulder and happened to see her look-alike being escorted by police.

In a matter of a few moments, Melanie found herself sitting on a plane flying to Switzerland with the Buffalo Ski Club. Reaching into her pocket, she pulled out her fortune cookie slip. It read, *You will travel on a wondrous adventure.*

An afterword to this story is on page 232.

24

OZ REVISTED
(AN INTERGALACTIC SUBDIVISION ODYSSEY)

by

Mary Agrusa

The rickety old farmhouse floated along gently through space, interrupted only by the occasional asteroid's brush, which shook its timbers to the core. Dust from exploded supernovas found its way through the gauzy curtains settling everywhere. Dorothy grabbed a rag and began her routine of clearing the sediment from the furniture. Since the storm that transported her home from Kansas to a deep space orbit, Dorothy's life was anything but normal. Most of the time she was alone. Recently Wendy and Peter from the movie *Pandemonium* had relocated to this intergalactic subdivision. Their occasional presence provided some relief to the intense isolation.

The big light was on now, flooding the house with illumination that made chores easier. Over time, its heat became oppressive; Dorothy's skin glistened as sweat beads formed and soaked the fibers of her cotton dress. It stuck to her like a clammy second skin. Looking out the window she spied Wendy and Peter floating by. She waved to her new friends.

"Sure is a hot one today, isn't it?" she called out.

"Yes, it is. Feels even warmer than usual, don't you think?" Wendy replied as he dabbed his face and neck with his handkerchief.

"Who knows how long it will last this time?" Dorothy replied.

"Have you seen Auntie Em or Toto?" Peter asked. Tying his scarf around his head for a sweatband, Peter looked like a ninja wannabe in a scout uniform.

"No, not for some time now." Dorothy said, "I hope they come back soon." She wiped her face with her apron and dried the trickle of a tear that formed in the corner of her eye.

The big light wasn't like the sun at home in Kansas. It was either on or off. It didn't rise or set. When it was on, it wasn't unusual for Dorothy's whole world to be literally shaken. People and things appeared and disappeared without rhyme or reason. How she longed to be back in the boring routine of life on the plains of Kansas.

Wendy and Peter waved goodbye as their home drifted away. Dorothy was thankful for that small dose of companionship and now the sting of loneliness was more pronounced. Who knew when she'd see anyone ever again?

* * *

Jack sat hunched over his desk and worked feverishly. His lamp was pulled down close to the paper providing additional light. The art room grew darker as the sun set and night began to fall.

"Are you still at it, man?" Tony, Jack's boss, entered the room on his way out and was surprised to find anyone still working. "I thought everyone had already left early to beat the Fourth of July holiday traffic rush."

"I'm so close to finishing this storyboard," Jack replied. "I wanted to get it done before I left."

Tony walked over and stood next to his artist and looked the drawings on the desk. "This is really good," he said. "I like the way you merged elements from the *Wizard of Oz* and *Pandemonium* into a sci-fi storyline. It's a new twist on an old theme."

"I hope they like the concept," Jack responded.

"Enough for now. Knock off and go home. Relax and enjoy some freedom from this place." Tony reached up and snapped off Jack's lamp.

Dorothy's world went dark. Residual ambient light provided enough visibility to let her find the couch where a pillow and blanket awaited. Without the big light there was little to do but sleep. She fluffed the pillow, lay down and pulled the blanket tightly around her. Maybe this time she'd dream of her old life in Kansas. It was unlucky not to say the magic words before falling asleep.

Softly she whispered, "There's no place like home. There's noo place like hoome. There's nooo pla......" It had worked once before, and perhaps this time when she woke up, it would work again.

An afterword to this story is on page 233.

CHAPTER THREE
CROWNS

25

FORSAKE THY BLOODLINE

by

Alli Vaughan

Anyone gazing out their window of a sky-ripped tower bordering the city of Mylain would see beyond the haze and fire-ash, the shining star, Avanara, hovering in the heavens. Only holy ones were able to ascend to this sacred planet, those with the silver blood line and it was required of all women of a certain age.

Maiden Amirya, with blood so silver it ran nearly white, didn't want to go to Avanara, though her ship left tomorrow night. The bishops living there were holy, but twisted by the energy source around which they lived, half humans, multi-eyed mutants with misshapen forms. The images she had seen of them in the holo-screen were like twisted nightmares and caused her night terrors as a child.

"What is power, Amirya?" Nalia asked as she tightened the golden crown of hair that ran rows over and over the small woman's head. Light trickled lazily in through the tower window.

Power's freedom, Amirya thought and then flinched. Nalia had always had a heavy hand at braiding.

"To not need power. To reach Mog'Ara." Her lips offered the ceremonial response but her heart ached.

"Again," Nalia barked, pulling harder.

Amirya blinked back tears. "Mog'Ara is power, ouch."

"Stop being such a baby," Nalia replied. "I wish I had your favor, that I could wear these crowns. I would endure a thousand hours of rough braiding if it meant I got to ascend. Old Nalia is stuck on the rotting planet for the rest of her years."

"You can take my place," Amirya joked. "To sit all my hours in prayer and attend to the bishops sounds dreadful. You go instead!"

"That isn't funny, girl! The Keepers could cut my throat if they even heard you saying that."

"I'm sorry, Nalia. It's just that my destiny has been sown for me and I'm not even the one holding the needle."

"You are one of the most powerful women in the world, Amirya."

But I'm not free, she thought dejectedly.

Later in mass, she sat with her head bowed. Next to her, another silver-blooded girl named Moyra sat. They had been seated in mass together for ten years, but hadn't spoken one word to one another. It was as if each knew that this time was precious, the other girls in pews ahead of them whispered and giggled back and forth during the four hour mass. Amirya looked forward to the peace and quiet afforded to these moments, the time she almost felt alone and free.

She almost didn't hear Moyra when she leaned over toward her and whispered.

"What will you bring?"

"Did you say something?" Amirya asked.

"What will you bring for relief?" the girl repeated.

"Relief? Oh you mean my one piece of home." She thought a moment. The other girls had probably decided years before, but picking one item to bring with her when she ascended made the journey a reality. Her own mother had brought a solid bluish metal sphere called a Cambrian, which stored thousands of photos for viewing. "I don't know," she replied. And back to silence the two went. Later, it seemed to Amirya that she had dreamed the other girl speaking.

That night was fitful and full of crying. Everything inside of her ached for a way out of living in the grotesque world of the holy ones. A figure approached her bed and broke her stream of tears.

"Nalia!"

"You haven't picked a relief item yet," Nalia whispered, "so I brought you this, a needle to sew your own fate." Amirya held the smooth syringe in her hand, filled with blood-red liquid.

"But this is!" Her mouth hung open a moment in elation.

"Yes." Nalia smiled through her tears.

"Oh Nalia!" She embraced the old women, a small gesture for the debt she'd never be able to repay.

With her golden braids woven into a thick crown, she stood in line the next day ready to board the ship. Amirya watched girl after girl pass through the gates and disappear onto the hulking vessel. As she waited, she gazed at the warning signs splashed with red letters hanging on the white washed walls.

Warning: Only Silver Bloods May Pass Through The Bio-Scan Force Field

When it was her turn, a voice addressed her in a stiff, bored tone. "Step through the scanner."

Amirya stepped forward, but the field became as impenetrable as a glass wall.

"Try again, please."

Stepping forward again, she encountered the same obstruction.

"What's going on?" a stuffy looking official asked, noticing the delay.

"There's been a mistake. This girl hasn't silver blood." A ripple of shock filled the air and the silence of held breathes hung like mist.

"Please leave the line and return to your home."

As she stepped out of line and walked back toward her quarters, all eyes followed her. Most eyes held sympathy, some superiority. One pair of eyes held sorrow. Moyra, the girl whom she sat beside in silence for ten years had finally realized the relief gift Amirya had chosen. Altered blood.

An afterword to this story is on page 222.

26

MORE THAN JUST WINDOW DRESSING

by

Connie Flanagan

When asked to name the activity I find most odious, I would have to say it is shopping. Thus it was that I was in a tyrannical mood on the evening in November when I went shopping with my friend Nadia for a gown to wear to my sister's upcoming wedding. Nadia had perhaps been the wrong person to ask for assistance as she loves shopping, especially for ultra-feminine attire. Her giddy mood served only to darken mine.

We had already been in four stores in which I'd found nothing appealing. Nadia prattled at my side while I looked gloomily into the display window of yet another store. The tableau caught my eye because of how real it appeared.

An exquisite mannequin with long dark hair and cornflower blue eyes was wearing a forest-green gown of velvet with gold embroidery. Her head was half-turned toward the window, as though something had caught her attention. Two other female mannequins, one on either side of her, were posed to appear as though they were putting finishing touches on the gown at the hem and the waist. Their garb couldn't possibly be described as formal attire: the dresses they wore, although pretty enough, were suggestive of a uniform of some nature. Across from the women sat a frowning, matronly mannequin in the most hideously lavish scarlet ruffles I'd ever seen.

Just as I was wondering what manner of shop this was, the dark-haired beauty turned to look straight at me and said, "You've been rather quiet tonight. Why so pensive, sister?"

I was suddenly aware of movement and noise all around me. Instead of the frigid November air, I felt warmth emanating from an enormous hearth in the perfumed room in which I found myself. I had time only to become aware of what I was wearing—a long beige gown with dark brown embroidery, unbearably cinched at the waist—before all eyes were on me. In addition to the women I'd noticed, there was also an elderly gentleman in what appeared to be some sort of military attire. Like the young woman speaking, his eyes were a vivid blue, and his beard and hair were a shade of grey like unpolished silver.

"Are you not happy for your sister's match?" the frowning matron demanded.

"I am, uh, well pleased," I responded, hastening to add, "Milady," when I saw her frown deepen.

The beauty and the gentleman both looked amused at my discomfiture. "I dare say we will find an equal match for you," the man said, smiling affectionately. I must have looked a complete fool as my mouth dropped. Marriage? Me? What form of madness had overcome him?

Shaking her gown out and dismissing her handmaidens with a wave, my sister approached me with her hands held out.

"The day Diana marries," she spoke, taking my hands into hers, "will be an extraordinary day indeed." She smiled warmly as she said this, so I knew no insult was intended. The older man hid a laugh by harrumphing into his beard, while the matron looked at me askance.

"If you ask me," she began, though no one had, "Diana's feminine attributes have been spoiled by her being allowed to dress in breeches and take part in hunting." She sniffed and turned to glare at her spouse, adding, "I dare say, no man values a woman who is better at bagging game than he is himself."

"Perhaps," my sister smiled warmly, "she will capture a man with her arrows. Is that not how Cupid captures his quarry?"

Before anyone could respond to this, a clamour outside caught everyone's attention. A young man, his uniform disheveled and torn, burst into the room. "Your Majesties," he exclaimed, "Something foul is afoot. The bridegroom arrives with his army!"

Indeed, the commotion outside sounded like a battle.

While the women froze, the king let out an expletive and dashed from the room. Without thinking, I hitched up my skirts and followed him. A few armed men dressed in the same livery as that of the man who'd interrupted us stood outside. None seemed to notice me, but the king was handed a sword and scabbard. Seeing some men emerging from a room down the hall, I headed straight for it, knowing that there I would find weapons.

Letting the men pass me, I entered the room and looked around. Immediately I saw what I needed: in the far right corner was a bow with a complement of arrows in a fawn-coloured quiver. Somehow I knew these were mine. Instead of heading downstairs into the battle, I rushed upstairs to the parapet, my blood thrilling.

For the next while, time ceased to exist as I loaded and reloaded, aiming at the attacking army. The king's men surrounding me were either unsurprised or did not notice me in the mayhem. I was alarmed, however, when my sister joined my side.

"You must take out their leader," she hissed. "He is disguised, but I recognise how he rides. There he is on the left flank, astride the piebald horse."

Implicitly trusting her judgment, I aimed carefully and took him down. It was some time before his army noticed and began to flee, dragging his carcass with them. After an initial sense of triumph, my heart fell. I had just killed my sister's betrothed! Beside me, she was pallid in her fine gown.

"Mother must never find out. But Diana, you have saved Father's crown!" Despite her pallor, her voice was strong. I knew that my royal sister did not disdain me but rather admired me.

"Diana, are you okay? Diana!"

I turned to face Nadia, who was shaking my arm. The window in front of me was simply dressed with plain-looking mannequins in wedding apparel. Where had the realistic tableau gone?

"Diana, maybe we should stop for a bite to eat," Nadia said with concern. "Your blood sugar must be low."

An afterword to this story is on page 224.

27

THE PREMIER OF WONDERLOVE

by
Todd Folstad

She sat looking out the enormous bay window, comfortably lounging in the long leather chair and she wondered. Wondering how long this would take. Wondering if it would be painful. Wondering if it would diminish her in some way to her people, her family, her lovers, and to her God.

She took another deep breath, savoring the sweet, almost candy-like quality of the air. She mused that the air doesn't, but maybe always should, smell this way. Almost like going back to childhood. Each sensation was new, each feeling deeper, each sound louder and clearer, each sight brighter and sharper. She felt as if she was being reborn with her fifty year-old memories intact. What a world we would live in if we could physically be eternally young and strong with our life-long learning still available to us.

A two-headed deer ran up to the window to feed out of the flowerbox that hung there. Its bright orange fur contrasted against the greenish tint of the Novermber sky here on Wonderlove. There were many opinions on why the sky looked as it did, mostly scientific and having to do with the combination of the planet's three suns. But she just liked the way it looked today, especially today, incredibly bright and sharp.

While she rested and breathed deeply in this wonderful concoction of air, her mind drifted to planetary issues. She had more than her share of challenges over the past two years as the newly elected ruler. Her people seemed to love her. She was a breath of fresh air to this once warring world.

She was the first woman elected not only to the office of Premier, but to any high office. There were no others in her cabinet, her parliament or any of the lower functionary segments of government anywhere on Wonderlove.

They had their first full year of peace in this her second year, and the global economy has come back strong. There was no question that a strong woman was best for this world where strong men had continually failed in the past. They were too quick to anger, too quick to jump and far too quick to battle. Peace was the only option that they never explored.

Now it was all they had and all they ever seemed to want.

A pretty young lady poked her head in the door to see if all was right and to see if the Premier required anything. She stated no, though commented, "I really need to have some of this air pumped into my office on a regular basis. It smells so sweet and my focus seems so sharp today."

The young lady replied, "I'll check with the office staff to see if that is possible, but I don't think you want this kind of air every day all the time. It might not be in your best interest to work in this type of an environment all the time."

The Premier chuckled and agreed. There would be others in her office that would want to be there all the time and she would certainly not get any work done.

She briefly nodded off, dreaming of her world, peaceful, respectful, full of good hard-working people and smiled to herself—she had done it.

She woke what seemed like hours later, only to look at the clock and notice it had been no more than twenty-five minutes. The windows seemed a few shades darker now, less light coming in, and her jaw seemed to ache just a little.

The door opened and in walked a very handsome young man, maybe in his mid-30's, in a long white coat. He was greying at the temples and looked very distinguished. "How are we doing, Madame Premier?"

"Fine, just fine, except for my jaw. It tingles a bit and feels just a bit sore."

"That's perfectly normal, especially after what you've been through today. Most people don't opt to have all of their wisdom teeth pulled on the same day they are receiving two major crowns on their back molars. That's quite a load. It makes even the most powerful people, powerless."

"I only have one question, Doctor. What do you put in the air here to make it so sweet?"

"Ah yes, my assistant commented that you enjoyed it—it's our sleeping gas. We use nitrous oxide with a bubble gum scent. It really helps when I'm working with younger patients. I was told that you'd like to pipe this air into your office. I'd caution against that—too much exposure can be very detrimental to getting anything done."

The Premier countered, "I can see your point, but wow, I could really get things done in this frame of mind."

"I suppose you have to get back now to the war preparations," stated the Doctor.

"I do," said the Premier." I had the most delicious dream under your gas that we were a world of total peace and that was the best dream I've had in ages."

An afterword to this story is on page 212.

28

DECK FIFTY-TWO

by

David Russell

My place has been crowded ever since I can remember, and I have lived globally. You may find me and my companions on a farm, small burb or town, park bench or palace, Regardless of setting, my status is regarded either as royalty or scum, lauded or passed off. There is no middle ground for me.

I like being in those social circles where big picture windows highlight a room, sun shining through, and I help my subjects find fame, fortune and maybe a little love if they indulge in enough libation. My friends, Jack and Ace, help seal the deal in these cases, and the king has grown accustom to my being a "player" of sorts, "worldly" as some call it.

Those situations where I am shunned leave me feeling anything but powerful or even capable of having any power. I am passed off, scoffed at, abused, and mocked. Even Protective Services or someone like phone psychologist Dr. Laura can do zilch for me in these cases. It sucks less than royalty. I much prefer the home where love abounds, a cruise ship where ambiance is plentiful, or being at a gaming table in top line casinos.

I was in one situation where I had met the person of my dreams or so I thought. Dressed in a herringbone suit jacket, he was charming, charismatic, and skillfully handled a pipe.

"I want to play another hand," he told the card dealer.

"This time I will go for 5 G. No more, no less," he added.

His hand was warm as he gently caressed the cards and of course, I was in the mix. I felt my heart begin to warm toward him.

I hoped he would hold me forever.

"Ahh. I have it. Playing it all," he announced.

Then it happened just like a thunder clap or a bolt of lightning flashing across the sky. I was done.

Minutes later he put down his hand: an 8, 9, 10, jack, queen, king, and ace. A straight! And so he won.

Instead of treating me like royalty, he treated me like crap, knocking over his $75 glass of wine on me and my companions. We were instantly disposed of. I saw him collect his winnings and beat it.

Oh, not to worry, my life keeps coming back and will do so as long as I am allowed to exist among the powerful and the seeming inchoate who play hearts like an infant bangs on a tabletop or a piano.

Yes, I am royalty in 21, poker, and other card games where I help complete a full house, and royal free in that game of hearts where I give the player who has me 13 points in the negative column.

You may have guessed my identity, or entertained me recently.

Try to consider my feelings next time we share whatever setting we are in.

If you care to know, I am the Queen of Spades. Please keep the light in that window!

An afterword to this story is on page 228.

29

WATCHER IN THE PLAZA

by

Karen Hopkins

The little girl stood at her window staring at the plaza across the busy street below. She wore her dress with the white lace. Yellow and red ribbons fluttered in the long black braids her mother had coiled on her head.

"Luisa!" She could hear her mother calling from downstairs. "Luisa? Where are you? Come now! We don't want to be late!"

Luisa frowned. She could stand at the window all day. She watched the old woman sitting under the flamboyant tree down in the plaza. The old woman was always there. Luisa scrunched her eyes shut.

She couldn't think of a time when she had not seen the woman. She was obviously an Indita. Her feet were wide and bare from a lifetime of walking without shoes. Her hair was braided, pulled tight, away from her increasingly high forehead. Unlike Luisa's hair, the old woman's braids formed a white crown. Her eyes were milky white from cataracts, though Luisa did not understand the natural cause for her supernatural stare.

Her huipil was worn, the embroidery threads hardly visible as anything more than colors and patterns worn into the cloth itself. It hung over the woman's three skirts, held by a wide sash woven with birds and flowers and fantastic animals, around her waist, nearly hidden by her bosom. At her feet was a small bag, woven of agave fiber. It stretched and shrank depending on what went in or out.

"Luisa!" her mother called again.

Luisa sighed and turned. "I'm coming."

She looked back in time to see the old woman raise her head and stare. Luisa could feel her eyes boring into her. She felt it as a physical sensation, a burning that ran through her nerves into every cell of her body. She pulled the drapes shut.

"Mother, who is that woman?"

"What woman?" Luisa's mother asked absentmindedly.

"That one, the one who sits in the plaza."

Her mother frowned. "I remember an old woman who used to sit under the tree when I was young. My friends said she was a witch. She's been gone forever, dear."

Luisa looked where her mother gestured. There she was, right where her mother pointed.

"No, mama look. She's there."

But her mother was in a hurry.

The next morning early Luisa slipped out of bed and downstairs. She stood barefoot on the cool tiles. In a few minutes her father came down the hallway, blowing across his coffee, balancing his hat and newspaper. When he opened the front door Luisa stepped out.

"Luisa, where are your shoes? Run back inside."

"In just a minute, Papa. I want to watch the town from our front step."

Her father was in a hurry. He gave his daughter a vague smile and a kiss and was off.

Luisa looked toward the church. There she was, seated as always under the tree. Today she seemed busy. She held something. What was it? Luisa walked out into the street toward the plaza.

Before she knew it she was standing beside the woman, watching the hands fly as she pulled a needle through and up and down, embroidering the front of another blouse, a huipil decorated with parrots.

Luisa clapped her hands in delight at the colorful birds and the old woman paused. Her hand came up and grasped Luisa by the wrist before she could move out of the way. Her grip was powerful, like an eagle's talons. She pulled the young girl forward. Luisa could feel the texture of the skirts and smell the old woman's breathe.

"You watch me child. Why?"

"Who are you?" Luisa asked. Her fear left her as the first soft syllables fell from the old woman's lips. She sounded ever so much like a bird.

"Who am I? Who do you think I am?"

Luisa whispered, close to the old one's ear. "I think you are the heart of the plaza, the soul of the tree. I think you have been here forever."

"And who has told you these things, child?"

"No one, Grandmother." Indeed, Luisa didn't know where the words had come from.

"I am the heart of the plaza. I am the soul of the tree. I am the first mother of the first son born to our people when we arrived in this land."

Luisa gasped. "And when was that, Grandmother?"

"Oh, that was many years ago, before this tree existed as a seed. It was before your ancestors came on ships to kill and then replace our rulers."

Luisa frowned. "Where did you sit before the tree was here?"

Laughter filled the air. "I was busy. I was a mother. I raised eleven children, a powerful number. I had work to do. And now? Now? I watch. The heart must keep beating. We mustn't let the plaza die."

Luisa looked around. The plaza was full of life. "How could it die?"

"It will die." The old woman was emphatic. "It dies when we forget. I hold the memories. I see the ones who come and go, so busy. But the secret of power is life. Many can no longer see me." She dropped the girl's wrist. "Take my hand child." Luisa shut her eyes. "My blood runs in your veins. One day you will sit here and I will be free to go."

"When?" Luisa asked simply.

"When? When you have lived life. When you hold enough power. When you have sweated and pushed and given birth. When you have laughed and played with your babies. When you have stumbled, blinded with tears as you bury your child, your husband, and your sons. On that day when you see that your blood and my blood run through all life on earth, your heart will be strong enough to hold the heart of the plaza. And on that day, child, I will be gone."

Louisa stood unmoving, paralyzed by thoughts of the future. How long she stood she could not say, but suddenly she heard a voice calling, a faint voice, faraway. "Luisa, Luisa, come here this instant!"

She started, her eyes opened and she saw her mother in the doorway. "Hurry dear. We mustn't be late."

Luisa began to move, but the old woman held out a hand. Luisa looked up and the woman smiled at her, a smile filled with warmth and wisdom, a smile that encompassed eternity.

"I'll be here until you're ready."

An afterword to this story is on page 234.

30

SUNSET CROWN

by
H. M. Schuldt

Ever so quietly, I closed my bedroom door and locked it. My heart pounded as I tried to hide from the intruder downstairs. Stepping across the room, I crept toward an open window and looked toward the ground. The glass had broken during the explosions, and I couldn't get rid of a nervous feeling that took over in my body.

Can it hear me? Can machines hear?

Every fiber in me wanted to cry out for help.

What is causing this rumbling outside? Where are the police?

I heard unusual sounds in my neighborhood, the sounds of motors and gears and horrible screeching levers.

I peered cautiously out my bedroom window. Two houses blazed furiously. Smoke billowed from the ground rising into a gray sky, hiding large portions of what was once fresh and blue from earlier that day. My next-door neighbor's car lay upside down in the lawn. A car alarm was ringing off in the distance and roofs scattered the ground endlessly. No bird or creature stirred about, only the dreadful movement of unmerciful machines. Large and small moving mechanical killers had attacked us. Houses were lighting on fire, which made terrible havoc on my street, but somehow I survived. It was only a matter of time. My house was sure to be next.

Desperate, I looked down Susie Brumley Place to find any sign of life.

Is the air even safe to breathe?

I was deeply troubled by a thick atmosphere until I saw movement in an open garage across the street. It was a person, a human, my neighbor Dan. A large hardcover book lay on the ground near my feet, my Webster Dictionary. Picking it up, I held tight to one end and swung at the broken window. A piece of glass broke off and fell onto an overhang. Dan looked up.

Certainly Dan looked in my direction and soon made his way over. He turned his head in search of any sign of the intruders. Once near enough to my window, he spoke intently, "Kelly! Does your car have gas? My tank is almost empty."

"I have a full tank," I said. He wanted my car and I was determined to go with him. He wasn't the type to leave me behind since, just the week before, he had rung my doorbell trying to convince me to invest in a bug-out bag.

"Did a machine get in your house?" Dan asked.

"Something's downstairs," I said. "It's moving. I have to jump."

"I can catch you," he said with confidence. "Can you bring your car key?"

I gave him a look of uncertainty. Scanning the room, I found my purse. A loud bang on my door caused me to tremble uncomfortably. My hands felt panicky searching but I found my keys and placed them in my jean pocket.

Dan was urgent. "You have to trust me. I'll catch you."

Another pounding sound startled me, coming from the other side of my bedroom door. I had no other choice. I tossed my purse to the ground and climbed through the opening. Kneeling down next to the overhang, the gutter felt flimsy as if it wouldn't hold my weight.

"Don't think about it," he said.

I hung only for a brief moment until the gutter broke. He cushioned my fall the best he could and we went tumbling down on the grass.

"You okay?" he asked.

"I think so."

We ran toward my garage and I entered the code. The door went up and we slid into the front seat of my car. I started my car in the garage, fearing the intruder inside my house. Looking back, Dan and I saw another intruder, a large machine on four thick wheels, positioning itself in my driveway.

Dan and I knew what we had to do to get out, but he put it into words. "Run it over! Don't think about it!"

The impact crashed heavy against the machine, causing temporary malfunction on the intruder's part. Once I shifted my car from reverse to drive, I sped toward the interstate. The other intruders were the strangest looking creatures with odd-looking robot-machines, and they were either roaming on foot in my neighborhood or driving white vans that had no windows in the back. The creatures were blowing down front doors with a single shot from the street, and they sent machines to set fire to the inside of the houses one at a time. We dodged bullets and rocket propelled grenades and explosions and then finally made it to the entrance ramp.

"Our neighborhood…it's gone." I said in disbelief. Ten SWAT team vehicles came from the north and passed by, evidently headed to our neighborhood, Brumley Hall.

"I think I know what they were looking for. I watched one of the creatures in my house to see what it was doing. It wanted my computer. And it might have been searching…for this." Dan said, reaching into his backpack—his bug-out bag. He pulled out a gold crown fit for a king.

"Will they follow us?" I asked, believing that Dan had some type of inside knowledge about the future. I was both uneasy and comforted that Dan didn't like to play by the rules. Even though he made several neighbors upset by his blunt remarks and rough edges, I knew he meant well. Did he really know what he was talking about?

"I need to get a few things back home," I said.

"You ain't got a home. Before the machine blew down my door, I did a wireless search on a database in one of the white vans. It was programmed to attack our entire neighborhood. The machines are programmed. But their intelligence is limited," Dan said.

"Where do we go?" I asked.

"We have to find a window facing west," he said. "It has to be on the west side of a building."

"What?" I asked.

This discussion in my car changed my life as much as the total destruction of my neighborhood. Dan read an inscription on the inside of the crown:

Your final destination
At sunrise you can see.

With a crown in position and

A window facing east,

You will receive hope for each new day.

Machines are programmed and

They process commands, but

Your weapon is understanding.

A window facing west

Gives you knowledge for every step.

It was the most unusual thing to hear Dan speak about the vision he saw through his kitchen window. He told me that at sunset the night before, he had placed the crown on his head and looked out his window facing west, and to his great surprise, he saw a location of where he was to go next - my house. It seemed impossible, but I had to take his word for it.

The sun sank lower and lower to our left, and it was about to touch down on the horizon. So we pulled into a motel parking lot. Briskly walking inside, we tried to blend in as regular people.

Two others sat separately in a small cafeteria. An old woman with thick glasses spoke on her cell phone while commenting about having no place to go. At another table, a businessman with a laptop stared into his screen as if the world around him did not exist.

Dan and I moved toward a window, beautifully open to an empty courtyard, as the sun was about to set. He pulled out the crown and carefully handed it to me.

"Only for the privileged," he said.

"Are you serious?" With an extra dose of curiosity, I took hold of this crown, noticing the splendor of its color and glorious craft. We stood silently, eager to see if it would show us a new destination. Never before had I worked so hard at trying to remain invisible. As the evening fell it began to get cold, and the full moon seemed to shine down onto the window as if it were a spotlight lighting the way for our next move. Finally the sun made contact with the horizon.

"Here it goes," I said. I placed the crown on my head and looked out across the patio. Suddenly the view changed.

"Do you recognize it?" Dan asked.

"The state capitol?" I asked.

"The capitol," Dan said. "Of course. It has a circuit shut down. The intruders won't be able to function at the capitol."

He was right. No one had been at the capitol in months, ever since the government collapsed and the circuit shut down.

An afterword to this story is on page 219.

31

WINDOW ON THE WORLD

by
D C Mills

Annabelle would spend hours every day sitting at the screen, staring at this the only window she had to the outside world, apparently unaware—or maybe just not caring—that the window went both ways and that she herself was under observation.

It had been this way for more than twenty years now, ever since she and her husband had been imprisoned in this remote wing of the basileia. Aldrytch was doubly imprisoned, not only physically in these rooms behind the force field barrier, but inside his mind as well. Annabelle's tears for her beloved had long since dried out, but her heart still ached when she looked at the shell of a man.

The continuous news feed now went to a glitzy glamour report. A celebrity party was under way, it seemed. Annabelle gave an involuntary start when she recognised the huge central courtyard of the selfsame basileia in which she lived, if this could be called living.

Hundreds of gaudily clad people were milling around down there, painted and bejewelled and obviously waiting for something spectacular to happen.

It was Aiken, she realised. Her nephew, Aldrytch's nephew, was twenty-one now, and this was his coming-of-age celebration. She remembered him as a newborn, just before everything had fallen to pieces.

Aldrytch was House leader back then, the most powerful man on Thessalia, in charge of one of the oldest and most prestigious Houses in the sub-sector. He had led the House and its dependents with generosity and care, using diplomacy to ensure peaceful relations with neighbouring Houses. Those had been good times, Annabelle thought.

But all this was not enough for his brother. Percival had wanted to enhance the reputation and glory of House Aiolos; to that end he wanted the power for himself—and he took it.

It turned out that he had plotted for a long time, not only hiring professional fighters but also persuading–bribing–a number of the House fylakes over to his side. In the ensuing struggles, many men were killed on both sides.

Annabelle had feared for the life of her little son and had somehow managed to get him on a ship off-world, with a large enough sum that he would be raised and educated far away from Percival's reach.

And far away from her.

Not a day went by, not an hour, when she didn't miss him. He would be a grown man by now, of course, and had probably long since forgotten all about his parents and his home world.

Meanwhile, Percival's son was coming into his inheritance.

She was distracted from her thoughts by a sound. Aldrytch was shuffling towards her and saying something. "The blood," he muttered. "The blood returns to the earth."

"Hello dear," she greeted him, as always hoping against hope that today he would recognise her.

"Blood and bone and filth and gold," he replied. "Land and sky. The void beckons. Death awaits."

"I'm sure you're right, darling."

The sight of the stefanet around his head, like a silver crown, suddenly sickened her. She had grown accustomed to it over the years, and on some days she didn't even notice it. Today, though, it seemed to gleam maliciously as if wanting to tighten itself even more, to dig deeper into his mind and destroy him completely.

For some obscure reason, Percival had not had either of them killed, once he had obtained power. Annabelle had expected it as a given and even made her peace with the supposed fact of her impending death; it didn't matter what happened to her as long as Jack was safely off-world.

But instead, they had been locked up in a distant wing of the basileia, to be guarded and waited upon by servitors and only ever seeing other humans on the big screen. The fylakes—now loyal to Percival—who had come to get them in the middle of the night had had their bolters set to stun, not kill, and when they came to, they were here. And Aldrytch had the psycho-mechanic stefanet fitted on his head, wires snaking into his brain.

At first they hadn't known its purpose. A tracking device, maybe? Or it might be connected to an invisible alarm, setting off a signal or giving an ambaric shock if he were to cross the fence.

In time, though, the effects became clear; Aldrytch began losing his memories, his coherence, his ability to reason. He never lost—or hadn't yet, at least—his speech or any physical function, for which they should be grateful, she supposed. But his mind was gone. Some days he would stare blankly at the wall for hours on end, completely ignoring her attempts to rouse him, to maybe go out into the pretty little rooftop garden they had. At other times, he would talk incessantly, rambling and incoherent, about gods knew what.

He had forgotten about Jack, too. She couldn't share her longing with him.

He was staring intently at the screen, and she turned her attention back to it to find out what so fascinated him.

The sacrifice was about to take place at the big ugly granite altar outside the basileia. The boy stood there—Aiken, the boy who was now to be a man, holding a long silver knife. Now he was stabbing the knife into the neck of an elegant chestnut stallion. Blood gushed out all over the boy, the altar, and the old priest. Annabelle shuddered. She had never liked Tyreesh'as, had always found him unnerving and sinister.

The ideograf suddenly swiveled to catch something else going on, something unexpected. For a brief moment, the rows of tiered guests like so many peacocks glided by, and then there was a young man standing there in the middle of everything.

Annabelle's heart stopped for a beat and painfully started again. She knew him. She knew this handsome young man wearing, incongruously, only one boot.

"Jack," she gasped.

Aldrytch looked at her shrewdly. "The blood returns," he said.

An afterword to this story is on page 227.

32

THE CROWN

by

Tom Russell

Most of the people in town thought he was crazy; watching as he spoke to himself. For those who chose to listen to him speak, they swear they could pick out two or three characters—I knew of four.

Justin Thompson was the third oldest child in a family of nine. His mom, stayed at home, tending to her baseball team. At least, that's what the townsfolk called the Thompsons as they rumbled through town in their station wagon with no muffler. Always the curious one, Justin's name was constantly yelled by his brothers and sisters: "C'mon slowpoke! Hurry!" they shouted in unison. "And pull up your socks, Justin. We can smell your stinky feet."

He was in his own world, fascinated by the colors and smells of a town that was rather colorless, void of distinction from any of the other towns in the county known as forty-mile, but it stunk. Goldville, was one of the towns that struck it rich—filthy rich. The town sat on a huge coal deposit that coughed out tons and tons of what the miners called black diamond.

In its heyday, Goldville was filled with saloons that stood shoulder to shoulder. The competition was vicious as women were brought in by the truckload to entertain hungry thoughts and to satisfy those moonlight desires. And then the need for coal waned, then died, leaving only the sour smell that permeated into the wood structures, trees and even the flowers that bloomed in the shadow of pallor.

During this time of lucidity, when everyone in town had focus, a common vision of working toward wealth, a young woman by the name of Victoria Swansong traipsed into town. She could unhinge the jaw of the toughest miner with her looks. It was an insult if she was called beautiful by men mired in lust. She considered herself far above those who chose to compete with her.

It took some of other women in town a few days to unveil their curiosity, to say hello, to somehow try to get a feel of who this petal was, but for the street-wise few, there was nothing but contempt. Like those who listen to the wind, Goldville, with all its wealth ascending from its bosom, Victoria heard whispers, promises of prosperity and the affluence she craved.

Soon, Victoria was the woman who could wake a tired night and fill it with laughter and revelry. The saloon owners began to pay her huge sums of money just to make an appearance in their drab, monotonous watering holes. Before long, each passing month of continuous carousing began to take a toll on her splendor until only one saloon kept her entertained—The Crown.

The Crown was named after a family of supposedly royals from England spent a night there, who claimed loudly that their crown was ripped off by a couple of hooligans. The saloon owner kicked them out into the streets, but not after hearing a litany of insults and what many believe was a curse:

"To the person in their right mind who wears this crown, their world will be turned up-side-down."

A few days later, after the indignant royal couple left town, a young boy had sold this crown to the bar owner. And there it hung, majestic in probable glory, in a place where the closest thing royal was the occasional flush in the never-ending poker game from those too old to work. No one ever really knew if the crown was real or not, or if the curse carried any truth, but, in time, the crown and the curse became real.

The Thompsons bought their groceries and loaded them in the back of the wagon. They counted heads and, of course, one was missing—Justin. They turned and saw him dancing near the old abandoned building with the words, The Crown, barely legible over cracked and faded paint. He was pointing inside the building, muttering words barely understandable.

Back in the day, there was no term or diagnosis for a person suffering from multiple personality disorder, they were simply called, for lack of a better description, crazy.

One voice, a young girl, cried out, "I want that! I want that!"

Another voice, a boy, shrieked, "Oh, shut your face. You can't have that. It's much too heavy for you."

"I want that! I want that!" continued the young girl.

"Shush, the both of you. You're going to wake him up. Shush," whispered the woman. "Oh, no, now you've done it. He's awake."

Justin continued to dance at the window. The voices coming from within were getting louder. "What are you guys looking at?" yelled the voice of an old man. "I'm trying to get some sleep here. What're you looking at?"

Justin's brothers and sisters surrounded him.

"What's the matter?" questioned his sister.

"Crown woman," blubbered Justin, still dancing, pointing inside. "Crown woman."

They dragged Justin away from the window to the station wagon. The family had one more stop to make. Their dad stopped to pick up a bottle of rum. When he got to his vehicle, his family was gone.

When The Crown was thriving, Victoria danced on the bar tables without a care in the world. She was a jewel, in a town dying a slow death. She would wear the crown hanging above the counter until one day, she went to sleep and never woke up. There she lay, on the bed, face-down in her pillow, the crown beside her head.

Her burial was attended by only a handful of mostly curious people. The police interrogated the other women in town, but couldn't find anything to act on. They simply labeled her death as natural; the townsfolk said she died from the curse.

When the dad found his family beside the abandoned saloon, they surrounded Justin who was wearing something on his head.

He spoke with one voice. "I found the crown."

An afterword to this story is on page 210.

33

AFTER THE FLOOD

by
A.A. Abbott

"Another drowned rat," old Seth observed as the door opened inwards and a man staggered inside.

"A pint of Mary's Best for me, Marilyn, and another for Seth," said the newcomer, shrugging off his sodden jacket and pushing his damp locks away from his forehead.

"Coming up, Brian," said Marilyn, pulling the first pint. "You're in the right place here. The water's rising."

"It was dry on St. Swithin's Day," said Brian, warming himself by the fire.

It was sizzling and spitting as flecks of rain found their way down the chimney.

"Chuck another log on there, Seth my darling, will you?" Marilyn said.

It was obvious he would do her bidding, as would any of the Crown's regulars. Marilyn ruled the pub with undisputed ease, her long blonde hair flying about her as she brewed beer and served it with big smiles and bigger sandwiches. Her charm and self-assurance were useless in the face of Mother Nature, though, and the saints fared no better.

"Summer's over. St. Swithin has no sway now." She shuddered as she heard the window frames rattle and the rain lash at the glass. The leaded windows themselves were almost dark, the stained glass crowns within them a dull sludgy brown, when usually they caught the sunlight and glinted like gold and red jewels.

The pub stood on a granite outcrop above the surrounding lowlands. Although the old marshes had been drained two centuries ago, they had still flooded in Marilyn's lifetime and doubtless would again, one day.

Perhaps that day had arrived. As the light dimmed still further and the wind howled, the stone building filled. Men, women and children from the farms, even the mayor and villagers of the small hamlet at the foot of the granite rise, turned up with torches, food and spare clothing. Marilyn, a frown suddenly aging her beyond her forty years, brought sandbags from the cellar.

"You want those round the doors?" the mayor asked.

"Yes please, Bill." Her smile was wide and grateful. "I think we'll lock them after that."

"What about the cellar?"

"It's lined and watertight."

"She likes to be busy, doesn't she?" Bill said, looking above the bar at a framed picture of twin teenage girls, standing in front of a mellow sandstone wall. An inn sign, with a painting of a golden crown, could just be seen above their heads. They were both smiling to the camera, holding hands, blonde heads glinting in the sun and revealing not a care in the world.

Brian grunted.

It was pitch black now, and still the wind moaned and eddied around the building, like a huge marsh monster trying to grip it, pry it loose from the rock, and send it spinning into the rainclouds. As thunder roared and lightning flashed, there was a loud rapping at the window.

"Who could that be?" Bill asked. "Everyone from the village and the farms is here."

"We can't open that door," Marilyn said.

"The window." Despite the clamour of wind and rain, they heard the young female voice outside, clear as a bell.

"I'll do it." Brian was quick to volunteer, nimbly unfastening the catch. To his obvious surprise, a young man threw his body head-first through the tight opening.

"Why it's that policeman who stopped me on the motorway," Bill said, with undisguised disgust. "And I was only five miles an hour over the speed limit. I don't suppose you'll be going out in that unmarked car again anytime soon."

"Too true," admitted the man. "It was swept away when the river burst its banks, and I'd have been a goner too if it hadn't been for..."

Brian interrupted. "The girl! What about the girl?"

"Where did she go? Mary," said the policeman. "Quick."

They peered out through the driving rain, seeing only the dark waters lapping at the doorstep.

"Where is she?" Brian asked. "Why didn't you send her through the window before you? Women and children first, surely?"

The other man looked dazed. "She wouldn't let me. I begged her, tried to push her, even, told her that raft of hers was too flimsy. It seemed ready to disintegrate at any moment. I can't believe it really brought us here."

"Call yourself a man," Bill muttered.

"What sort of license does this pub have?" the policeman asked sharply, giving the evil eye to the mayor. "It's after midnight. Nobody should be drinking by now."

"Tell you what," said the mayor, "You don't ask anyone that question and we won't tell anyone that you left a girl to drown out there."

"There's nothing to tell," old Seth said. "You know that, Bill. Brian, look."

Marilyn was staring at the picture of the two girls, quietly sobbing.

"Why, that's Mary," the policeman cried, pointing.

"Marilyn's twin," said old Seth, crossing himself. "She died in the last flood, a quarter century ago."

An afterword to this story is on page 235.

34

FOR THE LOVE OF VASHTI

by

Sylvia Stein

It has been said that in 18th century England there lived a strong knight named Mikos who was deeply in love with a beautiful princess by the name of Vashti. He thought of her very often and he wanted so much for her to return his love.

Surprisingly, Vashti began to develop a deep love for him and this made Mikos very happy. Unfortunately, their love was cursed from the beginning, for the beautiful princess was supposed to marry the King of Essex in the royal Kingdom of Barrantia. Vashti began to envision herself as a woman who was trapped with no power to choose the man of her dreams. She would sit by her window and cry herself to sleep.

"Oh, Mikos," Vashti spoke softly to herself. "I love you and I do not understand why my father insists on this."

Early the next morning, Vashti approached her father and pleaded. "Father, we must speak now. Why are you forcing me to marry someone I barely know?"

"My dear daughter, Vashti, we have been through this many times. Armand is King of Essex and he has chosen you to be his queen. You must take him to be your husband. Besides, you will wear the one and only crown passed on from his grandmother, Queen Lizania."

In the land of Essex, King Armand stood next to a woman by the name of Malandria who was in love with him. Malandria, in her bewitching ways, set out her plan to become the next queen. Malandria was a royal maiden who had been told, ever since she was a young girl, that she would become a queen. Sadly, for Malandria, Armand fell in love with the beauty of Vashti and he wanted to marry her instead.

There was just one last thing for Malandria to do to distract the king and stall for time. She called for the help of her servant, Archibald. He was so in love with her that he would do anything for her.

"Yes, Malandria, my fair maiden!" Archibald said eagerly.

"I need for you to steal the crown of Queen Lizania," she said.

"But, Your Grace, that is impossible."

"Now, Archibald, do you really want to disappoint me?"

"No. No. I will find a way to get you the crown, Your Grace."

"One moment, Archibald. I need another favor," she smirked. "I need for you to take it to Lord Baine's chambers. King Armand will think he stole the crown."

"As you wish," he smiled.

Luckily for Lord Baine, Archibald was very grateful to him for all he had done to help him, and Archibald was not about to betray Lord Baine. Instead, Archibald decided to place the crown in Malandria's room and have King Armand decide her fate.

However, what Archibald did not know was that Vashti's heart belonged to Mikos. And as the days grew closer to the wedding, Vashti's hope for her father to let her be with whom she wanted to be with was impossible.

Mikos overheard the news of the pending nuptials and he was more convinced than ever that there was nothing he could do to stop them. *Oh my dearest Vashti, this will not be easy for me but I will not cause any trouble for you. I must let you go.*

It did not take long for King Armand to learn that the crown was missing. The most puzzling part was that the king was not surprised. He told his knights that he would be handling the matter personally.

Malandria was overjoyed when Archibald told her that the king had asked to see her. Malandria had dreamed of this day since she was a young girl. She could not help but grin from ear to ear as she walked towards him.

"Oh, Armand," she smiled.

"Please, Malandria, stop this now," he lashed out. "I know what you have done."

"Whatever do you mean?"

"I know you have taken my grandmother's crown and that you have it hidden in your room."

"That is absurd. I will not tolerate this. I did not hide Queen Lizania's crown in my room!"

"Archibald!" called King Armand.

"Yes, Your Majesty!" the servant said nervously.

"Can you show me where Malandria hid the crown?"

Archibald stepped out and led him to where the crown was hidden—in Malandria's room. Malandria began to scream.

"Malandria!" the king cried out in anger. "You will be banished to another kingdom for your crime! Archibald, you can come and work for me and be my new queen's servant."

"Armand, please," she cried. "You know I have always loved you!"

"I am sorry, Malandria, but my heart belongs to another."

Once the crown was found, King Armand was anxious to marry the beautiful Vashti. As the time of the royal wedding neared, Mikos decided to go to another country. He left a message with another servant and had it delivered to Vashti. She was devastated when she received the message.

News of Vashti's love circled around the Kingdoms of Essex and Barrantia. Then the time came when King Armand decided to see his future bride.

"King Armand, you are not supposed to be here!" she exclaimed.

"My beloved Vashti, I have come to see you in person to let you know that I will not be marrying you."

"Whatever do you mean?" Vashti asked, looking surprised.

"Vashti, you do not love me. And as much as I love you, I have to let you be happy."

At this moment, Vashti could not believe her ears. King Armand was so vulnerable and this made her have a change of heart. "Listen, King Armand. I may not love you now but I can learn to do so."

"But your heart belongs to Mikos."

"Yes."

"Then go."

"But what about you?"

"No need to worry about me."

"You understand then."

"Yes. You must find him."

"I will do as you say."

At that moment, Mikos came through the door. Once King Armand saw Mikos and Vashti gaze at one another, he began to walk out the door.

"Go ahead. Be happy!" the king said, and then he left the room.

Finally, Vashti and Mikos embraced.

An afterword to this story is on page 214.

35

REBEL KING

by
Lynette White

Staring out the window, Robert's strong body was so still it resembled the marble statue just an arm's length away. The breeze playing with his freshly cut brown hair was ignored. His muscles, aching from the prolonged fixed stance, were not acknowledged. Robert Livingston, Duke of Abbington, was stripped of his title, his lands, and his wealth because he dared to openly take a stand against the crown. Now marked as a fugitive, Robert depended on the rebels to keep him hidden from the king's soldiers.

The middle-aged Friar Shea cautiously walked into the room of the stately country cottage, home of the Duke of Errington. It was a dangerous risk the friar and the Duke were willing to take, being loyal to Robert and his princess bride. Friar Shea's wiry body paused to study the young duke. He quietly moved forward and was nearly upon Robert before the ousted duke spun around, dagger at the ready. Stopping himself just short of attacking the good friar, Robert blushed.

"Friar Shea, I am so sorry," he apologized.

Friar Shea smiled graciously and lowered his head. "I am the one who must apologize, My Lord. I should have alerted you of my presence."

Turning back toward the window, Robert sighed. "I am nothing more than a common man. King Henry saw to that."

"A title does not constitute a man's worth, Robert Livingston. King Henry has proven that as well."

Robert chuckled, "Indeed he has."

"Why so melancholy on the eve before your wedding?" the Friar queried. "Do you question yourself?"

Robert shook his head. "Of course not, Friar. I have loved Claudette since we were children," he answered and turned away from the window.

"But, what do I have to offer her as a life, Friar Shea? I am a fugitive with no home, no money, no title, nothing. She is the king's daughter."

"Who was declared a traitor because, like you, she dared to challenge her father," Friar Shea pointed out. "If it were not for you, she would have died today. Instead, she is getting married tomorrow to her brave knight. So, what did her priceless crown get her? She is a fugitive. Just as you are."

Robert walked past him. "I suppose so. But, where does this leave us, Friar? Where do we go from here?"

The friar tapped his chin thoughtfully for a moment. Pointing at Robert he issued the challenge, "Where do you want it to go, ought to be the better question. People will wonder if you marry the princess because of *who* she is or *what* she is. Do you cherish her love, Robert of Abbington? Or, do you covet your own crown?"

Robert's eyes narrowed. "What do you think, Friar?" he pushed back.

The good priest was unmoved. "I think you cherish her love. I know you do not covet the throne, but you would not refuse it either. You are a man of ambition, but you do not squander that ambition."

Robert clicked his tongue. "Always the man with the ambiguous answers. Yet, I still trust you."

"Because in your heart, you know I will never give you a reason to question that trust." The Friar assured him. Robert nodded and moved back to the window.

A long silence followed before Friar Shea spoke again. "The country is becoming divided as word spreads of your daring rescue, and the king's actions against his own daughter. King Henry was doing a good job of keeping Claudette's whereabouts a secret until *you* stormed the palace dungeons two weeks ago. The truth behind her death was intended to be kept a secret. The official announcement was to be that she died from an unexplained illness."

"I must warn you that King Henry has vowed to stop at nothing now until both you and Claudette are dead. On the other hand, your bold disregard for the king has endeared you to the rebel forces. In fact, there are some who have named you the *Rebel King*."

"Thanks to you, those who oppose King Henry have all the fuel they need now to spread their discontent. Once word spreads that you have taken Claudette as your wife, it will unleash a storm I pray you are prepared for."

Friar Shea paused for a moment, his gaze becoming stern. "My question to you again, Robert, is where do you *want* this to go? Have you chosen to spend your life as a fugitive? Or, do you seek King Henry's throne?"

Robert remained silent for several moments before answering. "I am not the one who needs to sit on the throne as king, Friar, but Claudette needs to be queen. She is the only one who can reverse the damage Henry has caused. That leaves me with two options. I take her as my wife and seek to overthrow King Henry. Or, I walk away from this, leaving Claudette to walk this treacherous path alone."

"And your choice?"

Robert smiled and shrugged. "My heart set my course years ago, Friar. Therefore, I will take Claudette as my wife tomorrow and pay the consequence for that decision as it manifests itself."

The friar's lips curled up into a smile. "Ah, the price of love. That is why I took the coward's way out and became a priest."

Both men laughed and for a moment the burden was lighter. Friar Shea patted Robert on the shoulder. "Get some rest, My Lord. We will address your path to the throne another day."

An afterword to this story is on page 223.

36

THE CROWN OF THORNS

by
Craig Teal

Sophie awoke with a start. She felt stillness in the air and a presence as though someone was watching her. Listening intently, she slowly sat herself up within her bed, edging her feet slowly to the floor. She shuddered as her bare feet hit the cold floor as she rose from the warm covers of her bed.

Sophie stopped for a moment as she realised that her room seemed to appear devoid of all life and colour. Even her carriage clock seemed fixed in a moment of time. It was only when Sophie stopped for a moment to comprehend if she was dreaming, that she saw it. A single figure stood in the dark of the hallway beyond her bedroom door, motionless and staring directly at her.

With a dry mouth Sophie called out to her visitor, "Who are you?"

The figure appeared to reply but Sophie heard no response. Feeling her resolve grow, Sophie took another step forward.

"I asked you who are you," she repeated again, her tone this time bolstered by her confidence. Again the figure replied but Sophie heard no answer.

"Answer me!" she shouted.

She moved out of her room, and her anger was quickly replaced with shock. Across the landing from her appeared her very likeness, wearing a gown of silver and gold. Upon her head she wore a crown of golden thorns.

"It's not you," a deep voice spoke out, shaking Sophie from her shock as she spun to her right. There at the end of the landing stood a man in a grey suit. "They always think it's themselves" he mused as he produced a pack of cigarettes from his pocket "which of course is understandable, considering the circumstances we find ourselves in." He lit the cigarette.

"Who are you?" Sophia stuttered at the presence of the man, her eyes quickly searching for something to use as a weapon.

"Who I am is of little consequence," he continued, before pointing the crown on the head of Sophie's likeness. "That, however, is of consequence." The tone of his voice carried with it a deep-set warning.

Sophie felt herself take a single step back and quickly lifted a glass ornament.

The dry feeling returned to Sophie's mouth as the figure took several steps forward. "You do not need to fear me," he calmly stated with a softer tone. "You may call me Greyson and I have little time." He coolly took another drag of his cigarette.

"The crown above her head is a much coveted and sought after relic." He paused as he watched Sophie's gaze return to her image. "Your great-grandfather gave it to me over a hundred years ago in order to keep it safe from those who would abuse its power."

"What!" Sophie cried her anger quickly returning "That's impossible, that would make you over a hundred years old."

"Indeed," came the response. "One hundred and eight years, if I remember correctly." Greyson slowly turned to her. "If you are so sure about what is impossible then answer me this." Again Sophie felt the weight of his words. "Why is it your great-grandmother wears the crown upon her head?"

Sophie's eyes snapped to the face of her likeness and only now did she see the face from her past amongst the age's pictures on her grandmother's wall, but now the crown was gone.

"It's time for you take your place, Sophie." Greyson's voice softened again. "It's time for you to go." His voice seemed to become distant.

"Go? Go where?" came Sophie's confused reply. "I don't understand what you're talking about."

"Take the crown to the Antiques store on Fisher Street. They will help you with what needs to be done." The voice of Greyson was now no more than a whisper as he turned and walked away, almost disappearing into the shadows at the end of her hallway along with her likeness on the wall.

A moment later, Sophie found herself alone on the landing, cold and very confused about whether she was dreaming or suffering a psychotic episode.

"What was that all about?" she mused as she put the ornament down and turned to return to her room, only to be confronted by the talk grey figure of Greyson. She yelped in fright and stood frozen as he leant down close to her face and whispered in her ear, "Aren't you forgetting something?" at which Sophie felt an intense pain in her hands. As she looked down, she found her bleeding hands tangled around the crown of golden thorns and this time Sophie did scream.

Sophie screamed herself awake from her dream, bolting upright in her bed, head arched and her heart was pounding as she looked at her hands. She let out a sigh of relief when she saw no blood or cuts.

"Only a dream," she sighed in relief, a relief however that was short-lived, for as she looked through her open doorway onto the landing, she saw her reflection in the silver full length mirror. Her mouth hung open, as upon her head sat a golden crown of thorns.

An afterword to this story is on page 236.

37

RAIN

by
Shae Hamrick

Marissa glanced out the window as the rain pounded against the pane. She should really close the shutters but couldn't force herself out of the warm chair near the hearth. She could call Amber but that would destroy the peace and quiet. Pulling the wool blanket tighter around her shoulders, Marissa decided just to leave it be. The castle walls kept most of the winds at bay anyway and this storm would soon pass as they all did.

Reaching to the table beside her, Marissa took the mug of hot kaffrin tea. Sipping the steaming dark brew, she remembered her first taste and not but several months had passed. Here in this same room at Fimos castle, she and King Celdane from Gre had spoken. He had returned across the waters to his own kingdom.

Glancing at the chair on the other side of her table, she sighed. Her face flushed and she looked around the empty room. Guilt panged at her chest. When had her thoughts for Farison become fewer than for this man? She smiled briefly as Celdane's face came to mind again, the concern feathered across his features the first time she had seen him. She cringed and shifted as the memory of the pain from the lashings and poison returned as well. Rubbing her throat a moment, she drank more steaming liquid to sooth the memory.

Farison was gone for more than a year. Would anyone fault her for letting go of her mourning and beginning to live again? Especially after the treason against her this winter? Oh this crown was such a burden. If Celdane had not chosen to rescue her, she would not have any of these worries now. But then neither would she have any of the joys.

Marissa picked up the parchment folded on her lap. Lord Kelvin's demand that she lay down the crown as Queen of Cryn and return to Ardon was tempting. It promised her safe passage. Yet he had also been one of the lords who conspired to kill her in the first place. What would he not do for the crown? How safe could his promise be?

If only Celdane were here to advise her. Marissa huffed. This was her kingdom and she was not about to step down now any more than she would have stepped down before they had tried to kill her. And after another king who had not known her had stepped in, risking his own life and people, how could she just walk away? No, neither Farison nor Celdane would have approved whether anyone else would understand or not. It was settled.

"Amber," she called loudly.

The door behind her swished and her maiden appeared at her side. "Yes, your majesty?"

"Send for a scribe and wake Lord Falon. I need to speak with him. And are those men of King Celdane's, Tomas and Emit, still around?"

Amber curtsied. "Yes, your majesty. Their ship leaves in the morning with the tide if the storm clears tonight."

Marissa nodded. "Good, I need to send a message with them. Please have the Captain of the Guards send for them."

Amber curtsied again and turned to go. Marissa glanced at the window and the rain.

"And, Amber," Marissa called, a smile playing across her face as she imagined Farison smiling and fading into the rain outside. "Close that window. I think we have had enough gloom and doom around here. It's time we get on with the living."

An afterword to this story is on page 237.

HEAVY HANGS THE HEAD

by

Randall Lemon

Conditions in Skaarzz had taken a turn for the worse and there seemed to be absolutely no way that the young Regent-in-Waiting, Sebastian could help. Years of drought and locust plagues had wiped out the economy of his kingdom. His father, King Hiram, had emptied the royal treasury trying to purchase those things that would help his people and his kingdom to survive. He had invested in new seed. He had brought in dowsers to use their arts to find hidden water. He had even paid rainmakers to come in and try to remedy the situation. But all his measures had proved fruitless and very expensive.

When things came to crisis, he purchased food and even water from neighboring kingdoms, none of which seemed to have shared much in Skaarzz's misfortune. The only things that remained of the Crown jewels were the actual crowns that Sebastian, Hiram and his wife, Junuvia wore.

Now Hiram had succumbed to a withering disease that seemed symbolic of the same withering that had destroyed the crops of the farmers. The King lay in a coma which is why Sebastian had moved from Prince to Regent-in-Waiting.

Denied the counsel of his father, Sebastian sought out his mother. He found Junuvia in the hallway behind the throne room. She had just called a halt to court for the day. When Hiram could no longer deal with the day-to-day matters of the kingdom, Junuvia assumed the mantle of power and had begun dispensing judgment in her husband's stead.

She had shown an amazing talent as a judge and arbitrator and the people had taken strength in her abilities. Sebastian often felt that all that kept Skaarzz from descending into chaos was the force of his mother's personality.

Sebastian approached his mother tentatively, "Mother, may I speak with you about the state of the kingdom?"

A sad smile crossed Junuvia's face. "Of course, my son, it seems that there is nothing else to talk about. May I hope that you have had an idea which will aid the kingdom?"

Sebastian had indeed had an idea but he had no idea how his mother would react to his plan. "Mother, all the people of our kingdom know that we are the nobles of our realm and that we rule here by tradition. Therefore I can see no reason why we really need our crowns. I was thinking that we could take and sell them to the merchants of distant Dandros."

Junuvia tousled the fair hair of her almost teenaged son. "Sebastian, your father and I had talked about precisely the same plan prior to his succumbing to the disease which has laid him low. All that the sale of the crowns would achieve is a delay of the inevitable; it would not solve the problem. In fact, we have decided that the problem is beyond our ability to solve."

Sebastian was shocked. He knew his mother to be a strong woman and it sounded like she was just giving up. "Mother, are you saying we should do nothing then?"

Junuvia reached out and patted her son's knee. "No, Sebastian. I am just saying that *we* cannot solve the problem. Our kingdom lacks the resources to survive these unnatural disasters on our own. I have hesitated to talk to you about this, because it will forever affect all of our lives in a most drastic fashion. But you are almost a man and we have brought you up to always put the good of the kingdom ahead of what is good for yourself. Can you do that now?"

Sebastian wondered what his Mother had in mind for he could see tears forming in her violet eyes and her voice had begun to quaver. "I promise you, Mother that I have learned the lessons you and Father taught me and am willing to do what is necessary. I swear it by the gods!"

The tears ran from Junuvia's violet eyes splashing down upon her bosom. "Then listen carefully my son and heed me. Know that your Father himself proposed this idea and that if there were any other way I would take it. I am a young woman still and many there are who find me comely. King Krader of Trentmoor is one such man. He has lusted for me since first he laid eyes upon me and has made known his desires on more than one state occasion. I mean to send him a message offering him my hand thus dissolving our kingdom here and making it a vassal state of Trentmoor. Then Krader will use the resources of Trentmoor to save our people."

Sebastian could hold back no longer. "Mother, your plan is impossible. You are already married to Father. You cannot have two husbands!"

Junuvia took both her son's hands in hers. "You are correct. I can only marry Krader if I am a widow. Your Father knew this and before he entered his coma, told me to end his suffering. I fear I cannot do this horrible thing by myself. As awful as it may seem, for the good of the Kingdom and its people, you need to come with me now to your father's chamber. We will say our goodbyes and then we will place a pillow over his face and send him on to meet the gods. It was his wish, my son. Help me fulfill it."

Sebastian wanted to scream. He wanted to beg his mother to forego this evil deed. But he had been taught well. Most people assumed that, because they held power, Nobles were among the happiest of people. But great power held great responsibility and sometimes provoked great sadness. He felt an overwhelming powerlessness as he trailed behind his Mother to say farewell to his father and perform this great sacrifice for the good of his people. Never had it been truer said. "Heavy hangs the head which wears the crown."

An afterword to this story is on page 213.

39

SHANALA

by
Robert A. Strobel

My name is Bobby Topanas. Topanas means "sleeping lion" in the Ute tongue. Topanas is the name my grandfather gave me when I was born. He told me he went on a vision quest and saw a mountain lion napping in the trees, hence the name Sleeping Lion. After having his vision, he returned from the sweat lodge. My mother then gave birth.

I just returned from my first year of college, in the summer of 2005. I am an eighteen-year old boy on summer break from Western State College in the mountain town of Gunnison, Colorado. I have had enough school for a while.

I've been out for a week, and during that seven days I explored the small canyon near our ranch. I live on the Ute Mountain reservation in Ignacio, on a ranch passed down through my family. I grew up on this land - I know every inch of it. As a child, I would prowl all over that canyon collecting lizards, snakes, turtles, virtually anything that moved. Mom would get so angry with me, she would go into my room to get my laundry and then suddenly a lizard, snake or some other denizen of the desert would come wriggling out from beneath the clothes laying on the floor.

"Bobby what are you doing, bringing these … animals in here?" Mom would yell at me and I would stand there with a "what, who me?" expression on my face.

Ever since her death, I have been considered the black sheep, because she was killed coming home to throw me a birthday party. Birthdays had been a big deal for my mother, not so much for me anymore. Every year since my mother's death, my father would go out to Red Feather's saloon and get rip-roaring, red-eyed, fire-spitting drunk. Then, he would come home and cry for hours. Dad was a very sad, lonely man. He gave up his spirit when the Chief of the Tribal Police, Scott Tall Bow, came over to the ranch and revealed that my mother had been killed. My father has not been happy ever since.

I also believed myself responsible for my mother's death. On my seventh birthday, Momma was driving home from the local Walmart where she had been getting things for my party, when a semi-truck ran into the side of her car. She was killed instantly. I was in therapy for a few years after that, unable to sleep and having bad dreams.

My father in all his indigenous wisdom sent me back east to live with my grandparents and complete my schooling. It was the pits. I stayed in a dormitory filled with nerds, geeks, egg-heads, and an assortment of know-it-alls. I was miserable there.

Our house was about a hundred feet away from the mouth of Winslow canyon. It was so small that it wasn't included in any maps of San Isabelle National Forest or any local property surveys. It has been called Winslow Canyon since 1848 when Bob Winslow discovered a gold nugget.

I knew that canyon like the face I see in the mirror. I have walked that land from rim to rim. Today something was different; the air was sweeter, the flowers were brighter, and I felt great, not a care in the world. Near a bend in the path along the water-worn wall, I saw a hole between the rocks. It had an opening just wide enough for a man of my frame to enter.

Dad used to take me spelunking (cave diving) with him all the time. My father told me that these caves were made by rushing waters millions of years ago. I climbed into the hole with a flashlight in my mouth. We never used any ropes when he and I went caving. He'd always say, "Ropes are for sissies." I agree with him. He used to say, "You must be one with the cave, feel her curves, contours. Be with her and she will show you her treasures."

I had a small flashlight attached to my key ring. I put it in my mouth, and into that hole I went. The cave began to vibrate. Suddenly, the walls began to convulse as if it were having a seizure. I lost my footing, I gasped, and the flashlight fell from my lips into a pit. Rocks and sand fell from the breaking ceiling. A rock hit me in the head. I lost consciousness.

When I woke, I was being cared for by a most beautiful woman. Her features were delicate and her skin was soft and smooth. Her eyes sparkled an emerald green hue, her long hair was the deepest jet. Upon her head rested a delicate crown. She leaned toward me and spoke.

"Are you all right, stranger?" asked the beguiling woman in a soft soothing voice.

"My name is Towei, Princess of Shanala. You gave us a tremendous fright when you crashed through our window."

156

I gathered my wits about myself and began trying to stand. I found that I could not. I stumbled and fell to the ground screaming. "My leg! It's broken!" I winced at the numbing pain.

Towei spoke to a small sparrow perched upon the sill of the window that I had crashed through. "This is a job for Phoenix our healer."

The sparrow quickly flew away and as he soared, I heard him speak. "Just as you ask, my Princess. Your wish is my command." The tiny bird flew into a great wall and vanished.

"Phoenix is our healer, he will be able to heal you. He is very good," assured the beautiful Princess.

She turned to a pair of wolves and barked. They entered into the hall where we stood. She then looked at the full length of my body and barked again. They left on a mission and returned, bringing with them a purple robe and a royal crown, setting it before Towei. The Princess placed the crown upon my head, looked to the wolves, and barked three times. Then they left.

A raccoon entered the large room, walked over to me, and sniffed. He reached to the top of my head, grasped a small tuft of hair sticking up and yanked it out. I felt no more pain.

I stood as if nothing happened.

I gazed into the bright green eyes of Princess Towei and asked, "Where am I?"

She then looked at me and whispered, "You are home, my prince. You are home, my prince." These words echoed through my head. I became light headed. Then, unconscious, my body began to shake and shudder.

"We got you now. You're gonna be fine. It is a good thing they found your keys," said the Emergency Medical

Technician. I looked up at the EMT. She was the vision of Princess Towei.

I could not speak loud but I tried. "Towei ... Towei?" I barely had the strength to croak out her name before I fell unconscious again.

The female EMT removed her helmet, revealing long silky black hair. She turned and a patch sewn on her jacket read TOWEI. Her lovely lips parted as she replied, "Yes?"

40

THE JIĂGŬ CROWN

by

Victor J. M. Christensen

"Good evening, Dr. Jones. How's the work on the Jiǎgǔ-crown progressing?"

"Ah, Mr. Zhang, good evening. We're following schedule quite perfectly. Have you brought Dr. Brody along with you?" Emma replied, trying to sound neutral.

"I'm here, honey," came the drawling voice of the American scientist.

It wasn't that Emma outright disliked Brody, but he was the one who'd gotten her involved in all of this in the first place. Convinced her to leave her work and life in London and go to China. She still vividly remembered when he first contacted her. She'd been woken up by a call at four o'clock in the morning, as if she hadn't needed more sleep. She'd been stressing about her Ph.D. defence all night and would have to do it properly without messing it up a few hours later. Brody had offered her a job, but she rejected it, saying that she already had an opportunity at the Imperial College after she received her Ph.D.

A few years later he'd shown up in person and given her all the details—or so she'd thought at the time and told her it all was arranged. She thought it was the opportunity of a lifetime, dropped everything, and went to China.

The crown-testing deadline was long overdue. It had to be finished and all the while she was missing London.

Brody was a bit old-fashioned. He wouldn't really let a woman run the show even though she was the genius they couldn't do without. He ran a comb through his white hair and sighed. "Emma, Emma, Emma, darling," he said. "Our employer really needs this work finished. Ain't that right, Mr. Zhang?"

"Please, call me Wei, and yes. My buyers need this product, and I need to give it to them."

"But we still need the last bit of testing done and we have to do it in the safest way possible," Emma responded. "I don't want any more incidents. These are human people we're testing on."

"Dr. Jones," Zhang smiled, patronisingly, "this is 2025. This is China. My customers are the American government as well as the Brits, the Germans, the Koreans, and of course the Chinese."

"Do you honestly think anyone gives a crap about a few people?" Brody interrupted. "Because if so, you're more naïve than you look. And that's saying a lot, Blondie."

Zhang smiled. "As Dr. Brody says, we need this. We need the future. We need the crown. We need the finished Jiǎgǔ Crown or Dreamcatcher or whatever you're calling it. Do you not realise how much money there is in the future? We have a window to see into the future. The future, Dr. Jones!"

"I know, but the people…without my research this never would have been made. You'd be nowhere. I didn't sign up to hurt innocent people. I signed up to create something that could be used to reveal a dream-like state in the subconscious—to access the mind's ability to view parts of the future, which occur while dreaming. We know this crown is more than a weird déjà vu. And we need to keep testing it, but I never…I never signed up to hurt innocent people. You! You're bloody out of control, is what!"

She had enough. She thought she was powerful and in control. But no, that was just an illusion to use her—to use her knowledge.

She left the office, slamming the door behind her. She went to the lab and quickly put the prototype in her bag, which she put over her shoulder. When she turned around, Brody was standing in the doorway. Judging from his facial expression, she didn't think he'd seen her put the prototype in her bag.

She glanced at the lab and quietly said, "I'll miss this place." Then she left, not breaking her stride as she walked past Brody and out the door.

"Dr. Jones!" Zhang's voice shouted behind her.

"Forget it, Wei. The girl's made up her mind," Brody said.

* * *

She was walking around downtown, not knowing what to do or where to go. She saw that Americans were following her, the CIA or some such. How could they not realise that a white man and a black man, both well over six feet, wearing woolen suits in the summer heat, would very easily stand out in China? She hadn't expected them to have backup, though. The British agents were better hidden—as well as the Chinese and German agents. She only ever came into contact with the Americans.

As she was walking down an alley, she suddenly heard the sound of coordinated running from men in suits (not a sound you hear very often, but very recognisable when you do). She quickly found herself surrounded by CIA agents. Then she was shoved into the back of a van and everything turned dark.

* * *

Emma was woken by the sound of a phone ringing. What time was it? What was going on?

"Just a dream," she murmured to herself. "I'm all right."

She looked at her alarm: 3:57:00 A.M. *Who would call at such a time?* Emma picked up the phone.

"Jones? Dr. Emma Jones?"

"I'm not a doctor yet. You can call me that in six hours or so if everything goes according to plan."

"All right, but I am speaking to Emma Jones, right?" The voice on the seemed stressed and sounded American.

Emma grunted.

"This is Dr. Brody, and I have a great opportunity for you in America. My employers are very interested in your theories on dreams, being a kind of window into the future, and I'd like to offer you a job. It's every scientist's dream, right? It's something to be remembered for. Imagine...what if we could know today what was going to happen in 2025?"

An afterword to this story is on page 238.

41

WHY WE FLY

by
Tim Girard

The flare arced high and fell into the trees, burning, brightly and leaving a streak in the sky.

Wounded, the lumbering bird cleared the treetops, wheels reaching from beneath the wings, engines sputtering and straining. The body of the plane was ripped and torn. The bodies inside the planes bore the metal and the fatigue. Shell casings and linkage sloshed around inside the belly of the plane. But the bomb bays were empty.

The mission for those returning was a success.

Touchdown. Rough and shoving, terra firma chiding and chastising the crew for thinking it wise to leave its safe embrace. The crew was home for now and the plane wheeled to its clearing, oil cooling and simmering. Nerves raw and bleeding.

The crew left its bombers, shaken and rattled. They were met with a chorus of hands, stretchers, and the shouts and orders of the medics. Ambulances opened, and they devoured the wounded, speeding them to a hopeful recovery. The not-so-wounded stretched their spent muscles and walked toward the barracks.

The crew then retreated to the little country home far removed from the fumes and machines of war for a bit of chow. They ate, but they did not say much, shaking off the high altitude freeze and the concussion of bombs below their feet. There wasn't much to say. Then gradually, a hint of conversation.

"That was a nice shot, tagging the wing like that."

"Thanks. Quick with the ammo. Appreciate it!"

"Guys, you remember back home?"

"Yeah. It wasn't that long ago."

"Remember cotton shirts and warm earth? Remember swimming holes and barefoot walks?

"Yeah, and I remember girls and warmer days. I remember the hot, hot summer days when we would hide in the swimming holes und under trees."

"Okay. Good. I want to make sure I ain't forgettin'."

"You ain't forgettin' nothin'. Same as always. We find the sky. We soar. When Jerry comes, we trade bullets. Our plane carries us. We drop bombs, and we make a fast path for home. Ma Deuce blazing and shoutin' at Jerry and him shoutin; back."

"Man, Jab, the way you talk about a fight, it sounds almost pleasant, like a little argument!"

"Skipper, ain't no other way to look at it! Jerry has his cannon and we got Ma Deuce! And Ma Deuce likes to put the kids in their place when they step out of line. You know the teeth of Ma Deuce are sharp!"

Skipper smiled gently, thinking about Ma Deuce—the big machine guns his plane sported. Her rounds were large, carnivorous teeth held together on a punishing belt. The guns growled those teeth at the German planes with violence and heat.

The Skipper's hands were on the yoke of the plane, not the machine gun. He had a strong, delicate hand that could steer his crew through vicious flack fields and land their plane, on two wheels and relatively intact. He was capable, and his crew adored him for it. He put his hands on the table and relaxed, because there was another mission down.

The Skipper called, "Find some rest. I'm here if you need me."

The crew patted Skipper on the shoulder padded by his flying jacket. Over the next half-hour, his crew left the hall, eager for sleep that helped them forget about the war that raged in Europe.

Skipper sat still, lost in thought. A young girl appeared near him. She leaned over and refilled his cup. His attention broken, Skipper smiled at her. "I think about you when I am in the air. I think about your brother. I think about the little kids living near the marshalling yards. I think about the mangling of tracks and digging holes with explosives. I think about the fires and how warm it is where they are and how cold it is where I am. I think and I think, but I try not to. Does that make sense?"

The girl frowned She reached into her pocket and fished about. She withdrew her hand and plunked a shabby sugar cube into Skipper's mug. "I think about sugar."

Skipper laughed heartily, though his heart ached. "Someday, my dear, I will drop chocolate bars instead of bombs! Then all the kids can have a taste."

The girl smiled sweetly. "Why? Why drop bombs at all?"

Skipper's brow furrowed, and his eyes glared. "A man with power has decided that the rest of the world should bow under his ambitious and oppressive ways. A man with a crown in our country has decided to take a stand against the tyrant. His decision means I make a decision. I know it doesn't make sense. It doesn't make sense to me either, but we have to stop the tyrant from making any more decisions. So we drop bombs and hope that will make him change his mind."

The girl stood tall on her toes and leaned toward Skipper. She tugged at a small cord hanging from his neck. "And this?"

Skipper smiled pleasantly. At the end of the cord was a little pouch. He withdrew the pouch. "That," he explained, "is everything an airman needs. The shell of an egg to remind us we were all young once. A piece of paper perfumed by a girl a girl to remind us that she waits at home for us. A small piece of earth to remind us to walk on the ground and keep our head out of the clouds."

The girl nodded, satisfied. She reached into her pocket again and brought out a small sliver of foil. She handed it to him.

"And this?"

"This," the girl explained, "is from a candy bar to remind you of all the kids everywhere."

Skipper reverently put the foil into his pouch. "And what shall I remember along with the kids?"

The girl thought for a long moment. When she looked into Skipper's eyes, she appeared old, wise, and from a distant land and time. "Remember liberty. It's why the bombs fall."

An afterword to this story is on page 239.

CHAPTER FOUR
ANOTHER WORLD

42

CASSIE'S CROWN

by
Lynn Johnston

Cleaning out the attic was a mundane task for Cassie, a sixty-five year old widow who felt useless if she wasn't productive. While pawing through a box of clothes, she ran across some soft leather gloves. She smiled as she fondly remembered the day Pete had given them to her for her birthday. Pete always had a way of making her feel special.

After her husband, Pete, died ten years ago, Cassie had resolved to live her life like a recluse. As a result of her behavior, friends eventually stopped coming by and neighbors discontinued checking on her. She was almost forgotten.

Even her children had little to do with her. Her daughter, Francine, was busy going to medical school during the day, working as a nurse at night, and taking care of twin boys in her spare time. Because they lived over a thousand miles away, it was difficult to get together. They preferred keeping in touch by means of technology such as Facebook, email, or texting. Since she did none of these, Cassie never knew what was going on with her daughter or her grandchildren.

Her son, William, was living as a missionary in some African country whose name she had forgotten. She had not heard from him in three years. She could only assume he was still alive with his wife, Lily. Last she heard they were busy forming a church and organizing methods for feeding starving children. As admirable as it seemed, Cassie resented the fact that he seem to care more for strangers than his own mother.

As she continued to embrace the gloves, pleasant memories poured into her head associated with Pete. Suddenly, in her mind she had stepped back in time to the day she turned fifty. Pete had thrown her a surprise birthday party! All of her close friends were there including her neighbors and the ladies from her church. Francine and William, who were teenagers, had both contributed to her party. Francine baked her cake while William had designed a special crown. "Put this crown on Mom," he had advised. "It will bring you special powers and everyone will adore you." She remembered placing it on her head and feeling very special. Was it the crown? Did it have special powers or was it just because she was celebrating her birthday?

With that thought, she put the gloves down and then began digging through an old dusty box. "Could it still be here after all these years?" she asked herself. Just then, she felt a slight prick to her finger. Smiling warmly, Cassie spotted the tip of a prong that had poked her while removing the scarf that concealed what she had sought. "Here it is!" she gasped while gently placing the crown on her head. Cassie stood up tall and erect and gazed about the attic.

Just then, she noticed a bright light glowing from a window. Balancing along the rafters, Cassie tried to quickly make her way to the window whose light seemed to be drawing her closer. Just before reaching, she slipped and bumped her head. With her eyes closed, she tried to compose herself while reaching for the windowsill. With a firm grasp, she managed to pull herself up to her knees. With her left hand planted firmly on the sill, she used her right hand to lift the window.

All of a sudden, the dimly lit attic became filled with brightness and sparkles that caused her eyes to blink as they adjusted. Startled by the sound of a loud *neigh*, she gazed up to find a beautiful white Pegasus standing in her attic with Pete mounted on his back!

With his arm extended, he called "Where to, my love?"

Taking Pete by the hand, she climbed onto the animal's back while trying to avoid harming the delicate feathers in its powerful wings. "Anywhere with you!" she answered exuberantly. With Cassie holding securely onto Pete, they darted magically out of the open window and entered a new world. Over a field of spectacular flowers of extraordinary size and beauty they flew. Cassie had never seen a more colorful and brilliant display of nature.

Shortly they arrived to a village where dozens of people stood as if waiting her arrival. With arms reaching upward, they all chanted, "Cassie, Cassie, Cassie!" Pete turned to her and asked, "What do you wish for, my dear? It's all up to you!"

A warm and enchanting feeling came over her. She closed her eyes again to capture the splendor of the moment. She could now hear familiar voices. It sounded like Francine and William.

"Momma, Momma! Are you okay?" she heard repeatedly. She felt the gentle touch of someone rubbing her back. Cassie slowly opened her eyes again. Gazing up, Cassie saw Francine standing over her. "Momma, thank God you are okay. What in the world are you doing in this dusty attic with a crown on your head?"

"I was just reminiscing the past," she answered. "Remember when William made this for me?"

"Yes of course," she said, taking her mother by the hand as she gingerly guided her across the rafters and down the steep attic stairs. Just before touching the ground, Cassie reached for her head, making sure the crown was still planted there.

Once her last foot hit the floor, she heard, "Happy Thanksgiving!" Cassie turned to find a room full of people. Francine's twin boys, William and Lily, the neighbors, her close friends, and ladies from the church were all there. The table was overflowing with Thanksgiving goodies such as turkey, stuffing, mashed potatoes, and pumpkin pies. Her wish had come true! Was this real? Was this caused by the some secret power embedded in the special crown? Cassie couldn't be sure...but she was certain not to remove it.

An afterword to this story is on page 232.

43

EMMA IN WONDERLAND

by

Gene Hilgreen

Outside, the sky was dank and chill. Tomorrow would be worse. Emma blocked out every other thought, as she paced back and forth on the deck. She was alone and she would be alone tomorrow. But if everything went perfect, she would join the inner circle.

She went through every detail of the plan in her head ten, twenty, thirty times. Her skill was meticulous. She would make one shot and the escape route she would follow. She had already memorized everything because she wanted to arrive at the point where she no longer had to think, just act. Every second was precious. One shot, one kill—she was ready.

Emma looked toward the entertainment room where all the members of The Corporation celebrated, including the inner circle. Not tonight for her, though. She would go to bed early. Six months earlier, Quantum Physicist Dr. Emma Dash had never handled a gun or a rifle. Tomorrow she would ace the sniper test and join the inner circle.

Tucked in her bed, she rolled through the channel guide. On the classics network, she found that *Alice in Wonderland* had started twenty minutes prior. She selected the movie, just in time for the tea party. Emma had read the book as a child and she knew the plot by heart. Gently closing her eyes, soon she was asleep.

In her dream, she was falling down a long hole—falling—then she rolled out into a room. There sitting at a cute little table sipping tea was a man with a tall hat and a big colorful bow tie. His face was painted like a clown. Emma giggled. The man looked just like her trainer, Jack. And the Cheshire cat who sipped tea with him looked a lot like Anna. Then she broke out laughing when the March Hare character, who looked a lot like Roy, pointed at her and said, "Why, look! We have company! It's Alice the Vixen."

Emma looked about the room and caught her appearance off the shiny wall. She was no longer in her fashionable leathers but donned in a pale blue puff dress, finished with a white smock. It appeared to her that most of the members of the inner circle were seated around the room as characters in a story.

"Oh no," she gasped. "You all think I'm Alice."

"Ask her, Hatter," the cat said. "Ask her a question."

"Alice, come join us at the table," the Hatter guy said.

"I'm not Alice. But I am a Vixen," she giggled. "I am Emma."

"Boo, hiss. Sit, young lady." This squeak came from a pint size man dressed like a king, wearing an oversized gold crown.

"Buck, is that you?" Emma asked.

"I am the King of Hearts," the King squeaked. "Sit. The Mad Hatter has a question for you."

"Why is a raven like a sniper rifle?" the Mad Hatter asked.

"I don't know," Emma said.

"Think," the King said.

"No, I give up," Alice replied. "What's the answer?"

"I haven't the slightest idea," the Mad Hatter said.

"Nor I," the March Hare said.

Alice sighed wearily. "I think you might do something better with the time than wasting it in asking riddles that have no answers."

At that moment the Queen entered the room. It was the queen no doubt in Emma's mind. The women wore the most beautiful gown Emma had ever seen. Her crown sparkled from all the diamonds. She was beautiful and everyone in the room cleared from her path. She pointed at Emma and uttered four words. "Off with her head."

"No! No! Char, it's me Emma. I know the answer."

"Off with her head!" the Queen cried.

"No! I know the answer! Why is a raven like a sniper rifle? They nevar (sic) put the wrong end in front!"

"Off with her head!" the Queen cried again.

"Noooo…I get it…they don't point the wrong waaaayyyy. They don't point the wrooong waaaayyyy. Wrooong waaaaayyyyyy. Waaaaaayyyyyy."

* * *

"Up and at 'em, Emma," Jack said. "Sniper test starts at 0500. Bad dream, huh?"

Emma awoke.

"Hey, Jack," Emma said. "No, I'm ready. Point it the right way. One shot—one kill."

"Ooh, rah. Right."

An afterword to this story is on page 220.

IN PURSUIT OF A
DWARF PLANET

by
Mirta Oliva

"I, Mary, take you, Johnny, for my lawful husband, to have and to hold, from this day forward…" A few minutes later, Mary and John had embarked in a very important journey: they had sealed their lives in marriage, and the vows they pronounced had come from the heart. They shared the same professional interests so a very promising future was ahead of them.

Back from their honeymoon, the couple moved to their ten-acre farm in Florida. The newly built house had a "lookout tower" on the third floor to house a telescope and other equipment. The four-window square structure was conveniently connected to the second-floor offices. As dedicated astronauts, they spent most of their spare time searching for earthlike planets in our galaxy. Mary, a very determined woman, was hoping that one day they both would be selected to explore one planet similar to ours. The only problem was that the planet had to exist and be found—a remote possibility. John, although somewhat skeptical, joined Mary in her efforts. The fact was that they both enjoyed this career-oriented hobby.

"Johnny, look! I think I have found us a new planet! Come here quick! It might disappear!"

"I am coming, honey! I am coming!" Her husband replied from downstairs.

"Oh, Lord, what have you found? I cannot believe this. It certainly looks like one of those dwarf planets."

"Johnny, let's name it MayTen since I found it in May and it may well be recognized as the tenth planet."

The young astronauts worked until late in the evening writing notes about Mary's important find. The next morning the couple went to work as usual, searching for any possible new findings by the space center's Kepler Observatory. They both were aware that under the privately funded space taxi agency, three companies had won space taxi contracts for the purpose of taking astronauts to orbit the Earth. Mary needed to talk to someone but, so far, she did not know where to start. It would have to be the person in charge of the Earth-orbiting program. In the meantime, Mary would gather more data on MayTen, the little planet, to add credibility to her discovery—as it would be presented to the pertinent official.

A few months passed and only Mary was selected to join and manage the first taxi mission. Johnny was happy for her since, after all, his wife was the one who had found the planet and was more interested than he was in seeing what was out there. The abundant private funding enabled the agency to go ahead with the project and, sooner than expected, Mary was already in space orbiting the earth.

After taking pictures and performing all scheduled duties, the group was ready to return with their paying guests on board; however, as the space taxi descended toward the earth a phenomenon occurred where it suddenly changed course landing slowly on the water, next to a small island. The astronauts had lost all communication with Earth and the craft's coordinates had been scrambled by some strange force, so they had no idea of what to do. Mary used all available equipment to explore the surroundings, to see if there was any sign that the nearby island was inhabited. For good or for worse, she observed a few natives on the shore hiding behind the bushes. As a couple of hours passed with no signs of any recovery effort, they decided to leave the vessel. Fearing for their lives but having no other option, they swam toward the island, bringing with them food and some trinkets as gifts for the natives.

"Hello friends!" Mary, all smiles, shouted at the natives. The men remained in guarded posture while the women and children began giggling. Upon reaching the shore, Mary offered gifts to the women. Apparently, they were friendly aborigines since they carried no arms and showed a passive attitude. In time, the men also approached the astronauts and guests and shared in the goodies.

Once they had socialized for a few minutes, the visitors were guided toward a clearing where women were dancing in circles. Mary, the only woman from the taxi experiment, was taken inside the circle and was crowned with a flower wreath. Mary did her best to dance, smile and sing to their tune, later on sharing food offerings of fruit and vegetables. All went well and soon the stranded visitors were taken to a hut.

Although Mary was trying to keep calm for the benefit of all, she was worried that she might never see her husband or family again. Now she was remorseful of having pressed hard to embark on her second most important life's journey—exploring MayTen. Oh, well…it was too late for lamenting or regretting. They had no choice but to wait for their recovery or to return to the vessel to try to contact the Agency. One thing that baffled them was the strange happening—the way their craft was diverted and brought down next to the island.

At nighttime, the natives retired and the group tried to get some sleep but soon they were surreptitiously scooped out of the hut and placed inside the taxi—off into space, all gears working again. At some point, the vessel was intercepted by the Agency. Hours later, they had arrived at the space center where the astronauts were separated from the guests for questioning. All on board agreed not to discuss with anyone the aftermath of the costly exploratory venture, following heavy interrogation by different government agencies.

Whatever happened during the MayTen mission will remain a secret but all aboard the space taxi believe that it was the work of extraterrestrials. While Mary would continue to search for any dwarf planets orbiting our Milky Way, she promised her husband that she would only join future space travels if he went with her.

An afterword to this story is on page 221.

45

THE EMPEROR

by

Joyce Shaughnessy

What fools they all are. If only they knew the actual power I possess.

I parade in front of cameras to make the impression that I am not the true ruler of my island nation in name only. I stand here in front of my bedroom window and watch my subjects going about their lives, and I know without a doubt that any one of them would gladly give his life for me. Every person I see has sworn allegiance to my sacred Imperial throne.

I love being the puppeteer of my government, carefully maneuvering every action taken. Even the person who thinks he has a hand in my political decisions does not truly know what the other hand is doing. When I agree to a move suggested by one of my advisors, he leaves me thinking I am in the palm of his hand, until his rival replaces him. No one controls my destiny. No one possesses freedom in my country, only allegiance to my uncontested throne through our national religion—Shinto, the Way of the Gods.

Only the foolish country adopts democracy. Who in his right mind would have agreed upon British Parliamentary and U.S. Constitutional rule? Both Great Britain and the United States are subject to the whims of its elected leaders. As such, they are weak and ineffectual. I will show the world how really weak the United States is. Before too long, it and other countries will fall at my feet.

When Nazi Germany foolishly signed the 1936 Anti-Comintern Pact with me, Hitler thought he could control me. No one controls me. I laughed so hard when Hitler announced that he would lessen the reins on the Aryan bloodline and agree to let Aryan Germans marry my country's citizens. Hitler must have felt awfully magnanimous at that moment. He has such high regard for his Aryans and now he allows their blood to mix with the untouched bloodline of my people. I laughed at the thought that Hitler would assume I would allow my citizens to breed with worthless Germans. It would weaken our bloodlines, our pure heritage. Hitler is a fool.

Hitler has been wasting precious time and money exterminating the Jews when he should have been utilizing them. His fanaticism will be his eventual downfall.

I don't take prisoners of war in order to exterminate them, unless it amuses me. I do, however, work them until they die. I will make them my slaves, not simply eradicate them. Prisoners will be eventually eliminated, but first they will work my mines and my factories until they can no longer move, until their wasted bodies lay to rot in the ground.

When I attacked Mongolia, Hitler was so angry that he almost had a stroke. I laughed at his naivety. Why should I not conquer the weakened and ineffectual Chinese? He correctly realizes that I intend to conquer Russia after I conquer the Chinese, the islands in the Pacific, and, of course, the United States.

Once I control the United States and Russia, I will control the world. Hitler will fall at my feet. His people will die at the ends of my swords, just as the Chinese are now.

Hitler thought I would not invade Russia when I signed his precious Anti-Comintern Pact. I do not keep agreements with any other country. In the end, I will enslave them all.

I am here to guide my people—the true rulers of the world—into the next century.

After all, I am the Son of God.

An afterword to this story is on page 209.

46

EVEN-STEVEN

by

Mary Agrusa

Lil T spied Princess Priscilla in the window, wearing a requisite tiara. The princess was reclining on a silk pillow—a picture of true royalty. Priscilla the royal Poodle was spoiled rotten, doted upon by the owners, Frederick and Ethel.

The royal owners usually appeared easy going and congenial, but Frederick and Ethel were known to harbor a dark side. The chill and extended hours of winter darkness set the couple off on murderous rampages. Frederick did the dirty work but Ethel was no innocent bystander.

"So far, so good," Sara the house cat said. "But you're not safe, Big Tom. You're an old gobbler. You need to hide."

Big Tom took Sara seriously and so he stayed out of sight, hoping to stay out of the mad couple's mind.

Rosco the Border Collie scratched his ear. "His majesty's got that crazed look in his eyes this morning. Good thing your dad made hisself scarce."

Lil T shuddered at the thought of losing Big Tom.

From around the side of Lil T's barn, Sara the house cat appeared wide-eyed with fear. She made a beeline toward her friends in the yard, crying. "Run for your lives!"

Rosco took off running on all fours toward the field but Lil T stood frozen in his tracks, three toes pointed forward on each leg.

"Quick! Over here!" Sara cried out from behind the hay bales, but the terrified youngster couldn't move.

Priscilla the Poodle barked out the order, her high-pitched voice was unmistakable. "Off with his head!" she cried. From inside the barn came the sound of a struggle.

Lil T heard a thud, and then all went silent. Slowly creeping toward the barn, he peered in an opening between two warped boards. Priscilla danced gleefully as Frederick lifted a lifeless gobbler in his arms. Lil T was horrified when he saw the mad king's newest victim. The corpse was Big Tom! Lil T peered around the edge of the building in time to see Frederick carrying his father into the big house.

The somber, dismal mood in the yard matched the grey winter sky. Rosco and Sara did their best to console their young friend. Lil T insisted on entering the barn despite the protests of his companions. The place bore evidence of a struggle. Big Tom hadn't gone down without a fight.

"What are they going to do with him?" Lil T asked.

"You don't want to know," Rosco replied.

"Yes, I do," Lil T insisted. "I have the right to know."

Sara lowered her eyes to avoid Lil T's gaze, and then she whispered. "They're going to eat him."

The thought of his father being used for food immediately nauseated the youngster. He'd never looked at the royals in the same way again. When he finally calmed down, he found a way to avenge his father's death.

The atmosphere inside the royal family's big house was festive. The table was set with bone china, crystal, linens, and real silverware. Frederick tucked his napkin into his shirt collar. Priscilla whimpered and barked, spinning circles of anticipation, which sent her tiara careening across the floor.

"Calm yourself, Pricilla. It's almost time to eat," Frederick said.

Suddenly Ethel entered the room carrying a platter piled high with turkey and dressing. She announced, "Thanksgiving dinner is now served."

Frederick and Ethel dined like royalty. Priscilla the Poodle stood on her hind legs waiting for Frederick to present her with a plate filled with turkey. Everyone ate until they were full. When all were satisfied, the table was cleared and the leftovers stored. Ethel noticed a car pass by while she rinsed the dishes.

"Frederick, who's that? I don't recognize that vehicle."

"Probably someone who's lost," he replied.

Comforted with his response, Ethel joined Frederick and the pampered Poodle who was reclining in the living room. She took her spot, pulled the lever, and raised the footrest. Frederick grabbed the TV remote to watch football. Before the first set of downs was complete, the turkey enzymes kicked in and all three were sound asleep.

So sound was their slumber that no one heard the creak of the old wooden steps out back or the squeak of the kitchen door when it slowly swung open. The click, click, click from claws on the kitchen linoleum also went undetected.

Happy and content, the royal trio dreamed in technicolor until suddenly everything went dark.

"Even-steven," Lil T said.

An afterword to this story is on page 233.

47

FAIR'S FAIR AT COUNTY FAIR

by
Shelly Heskett Harris

"If it's raining, it must be time for the fair," Martha Madison said. She was standing at the window in her daughter's bedroom, watching a raindrop slide down the glass.

Martha's daughter, Darlene, was slumped over the dressing table. "They'll move the pageant inside."

"Probably already done it, knowing Ms. Caufield. We'll take your dress on a hanger in a plastic bag. The first year I competed, the bodice of my dress was velvet and it water spotted."

"You won the next year?"

"Yes. And your Aunt Mae was crowned queen the next year," Martha smiled in remembrance.

"But Caufield took her crown away from her. Didn't she?"

"Oh, she tried but your grandfather was on the school board. It got nasty for a while. Ah, well, so many years ago. You're the first family member to compete since then. I hope the old bag doesn't try to pull anything."

"No one is going to catch me under the bleachers with some guy," Darlene laughed.

Martha also laughed. "Mae was sweet and fun but short on good sense."

Despite the rain, the parking lot at the fairgrounds was filling up fast. Activity around the field house confirmed that the beauty pageant had been moved into a building used for basketball. This location was used as an exhibit hall during the fair and rodeo. It was also used as a banquet hall for the annual Chamber of Commerce dinner.

"You're late!" Ms. Georgette Caufield yelled across the court at Martha and Darlene.

"Oh boy," Martha said under her breath. Then she spoke in a loud voice. "Ms. Caufield, dear, how have you been?"

Ms. Georgette Caufield was a short, round woman in sharp contrast to the tall willowy figures of the mother and daughter. She wore her hair pulled back severely and then twisted into a knot at the back of her neck. She looked up through metal rimmed glasses. "Your sense of time has not improved over the years nor have you seen fit to instill a proper regard for the niceties of life in your daughter." Caufield made sure the thirty contestants and various parents and volunteers could hear.

Martha kept a smile on her face but inside she was back in high school, blushing and feeling embarrassed.

Caufield turned her attention back to the placement of the flat bed. It held a hay wagon that served as a stage for the queen's contest.

"Let's go get a Coke," Martha said to her daughter. "Are the machines still in the back?"

"You cannot go!" Caufield interrupted. "As soon as I get the crown, we start."

Martha disregarded Caudfield's command. Hand in hand, the mother and daughter headed toward the concession alcove.

"If you're not back when I start...well, you're out of the pageant!" Caufield shouted. She hurried around the pickup, which was now backing up to the bleachers. The motor was so loud in the enclosed building that only the motor could be heard. While Martha and Darlene were getting a Coke, a loud popping sound came from one of the bleachers. Caufield was accidentally caught while the bleachers were being shoved against the back wall.

"Stop the dumb truck!" Caufield yelled, but the people ignored her.

Martha and Darlene, despite their act of defiance, hurried back with their Cokes. They stepped out of the alcove and saw Caufield with the crown in her hand. She was pinned between the stage and bleachers. The gristly scene was out of the truck driver's view. In fact, no one saw the trouble Caufield was in except Martha and Darlene.

"Oh no," Martha said. "What should we do?"

Caufield managed to stand up and scowl. "Stupid truck driver!"

Darlene stood there for a few seconds. "Well, we can't be late for the pageant."

"Right," Martha nodded, and the two crossed to the other side of the building where they joined the others and waited in line for the pageant to begin.

An afterword to this story is on page 231.

48

TALKIN' ABOUT MY DEFENESTRATION

by

Neil Carroll Ellison

She flew. The Queen actually flew.

Like the witch we all knew she was, Her Highness was suspended in the air surrounded by glass and wood. Resplendent in her most elegant finery, the Queen's robes billowed in the wind. Screaming at the gathering of peasants below her, she shouted commands and, pointing at each of us, demanded answers as she hovered.

Her mouth frothed and foamed. Medusian hair slithered in the air around her head. Wild eyes locked with ours. She was mentally recording every one of our faces. I imagined it was so that she could exact unspeakable abuses against us for our boldness in questioning her reign.

Her crown, also defying gravity, rose in an arc away from Her Royal Head.

On this gorgeous autumn day, thin clouds gave depth to her flight. Their languid, gossamer backdrop acted in stark contrast to her sheer bulk, making her seem more impressive. The Queen moved amongst them as though they were her servants. So as not to touch Her Royal Body, they separated to grant the Queen passage much as we did when she graced us with an appearance. The air and all of its elements belonged to her. Had the sky been merely a clear crystalline blue, her presence in it would have had less impact. I could not imagine an entrance with more panache.

She was elegant and inspiring. She was terrifying. She was....

f

a

l

l

i

n

g.

I shielded my children's faces before she hit the street. I know they wanted to see the climax of her descent, but I told them no. "Safety first," I said. "You wouldn't want to go blind if a splinter of her bones hit you in the eye, now would you?"

They petulantly agreed.

With a dull thud and swamping *bloosh*, the Red Queen lived up to her name. A younger, thinner queen would have made a more memorable noise. There was no dramatic snapping of bones, just the sound of a bag of meat bursting. It was a bit like one of our cows being stepped on by a giant or possibly a splash in reverse.

The spectators in the front row held up blankets to deflect Her Royal Remnants. Some entrepreneurial genius in the group had called it the "Splash Zone" and was charging a fee for what was an otherwise free gathering. They were having fun, experiencing the once-in-a-lifetime moment of sharing bodily fluids (other than the occasional gob of Her Royal Spit) with Her Highness. Various street artists feverishly drew souvenir sketches of the moment of impact. They could barely keep up with demand.

Years of living off of the peasants who begrudgingly gave her our fealty had made the Queen physically soft. Our labors kept us fit.

How else would our group have been able to move her fat butt out of that throne?

In contrast to the Queen's thunderous arrival, her crown tinkled tinnily as it hit the cobbles. After bouncing and rolling a few feet, it spun upon itself in increasingly faster and smaller arcs; an anti-climactic drum roll announcing the end of the coup.

This was how her world ended: With a bang and a whimper.

A massive "Huzzah!" thundered through the crowd. Our fellow conspirators (those brave enough to have drawn the short straws) looked down upon us from the castle portal, which had moments before been a window. They looked tired in their triumph.

Willie rested on the stones, took a deep breath and weakly muttered. "I think I have a hernia."

Poor Willie. Always premature. We usually save the ball drop for New Year's Eve.

An afterword to this story is on page 225.

49

MISS BUBBLEKINS

by
Elaine Faber

Black Cat sat on the windowsill, staring at the driveway, waiting for Mrs. Stubblefield.

I should be happy Mrs. Stubblefield saw the lost and found poster and Angel's going home, but I'm not going with her.

Mrs. Stubblefield was sure Angel was her lost cat. Although Black Cat was also mentioned on the poster, she was equally sure that he was not her cat. Mrs. Stubblefield had reluctantly agreed to take Angel's kittens, but she wasn't interested in a stray black and white tomcat.

Tires crunched in the driveway. The dreaded moment was upon him. He was about to lose his Angel forever.

Black Cat's heart seized as the front door squeaked open, his heart pounding like a pile driver.

Mrs. Stubblefield wore her hair in a braid wound around her head like a crown. Miss Boopkins, her lost cat's name, was emblazoned on the side of a pink cat carrier and scrawled across her bosom on her tee shirt.

Black Cat growled, fighting the urge to tackle the woman…but he knew he couldn't. For Angel's sake, he'd put on a cheerful face. A bloody cat fight to the death wouldn't change anything Angel was leaving.

Mrs. Stubblefield hefted the cat carrier across the room, her face wreathed in smiles. She leaned over Angel's blanket.

The old witch! How dare she look so happy, when my heart is breaking?

Angel looked up into Mrs. Stubblefield eyes. Her face scrunched and she burst into tears. Tears of joy? Black Cat tried to be brave, but it was hard facing such a touching reunion.

If I stay another minute, I'm apt to bite her.

He sprinted out the door and over to the woodpile. There couldn't be a more miserable cat in the entire state of California. Suicidal thoughts one minute, and homicidal thoughts the next, raged through his breast.

I'll kill the old battleax before I let her take my Angel. No. I'll kill myself. No…her…

The child dashed onto the porch. "Black Cat. Come quick. Here kitty, kitty. Come back. I have something to tell you."

Yeah, right. As if he needed a lecture on civility while he watched Mrs. Stubblefield pop Angel into that ridiculous whore wagon she called a cat carrier. He flew off the woodpile, raced past the vineyard and then, skidded to a stop at the far edge.

Wait! I can't let her and the babies go like this. I have to say good-by and wish them a happy life. I have to tell her one more time how much I love her.

He slunk back across the yard, a defeated soul. He skulked across the porch and through the front door. "Angel, I…" What's this?

Mrs. Stubblefield sat on the rug cooing over the box of kittens.

What's going on here? How dare she look so happy in my moment of abject misery?

"Oh, there you are, Black Cat." The child's face lit up like a jack-o-lantern on a dark night. "Come and meet Mrs. Stubblefield. She says she made a mistake. Angel isn't her lost cat after all, but she wants to take the little cream sister home. Isn't that wonderful?"

A beam of sunshine shimmered through the window, forming a halo around Angel's head. Angel's not her cat? She's not leaving? Hallelujah! Mrs. Stubblefield stroked the kitten with one finger. "I think I'll call you…Miss Bubblekins…Yes, dats dust what I'll call you."

Black Cat shuddered. *Who would think I would welcome the day a daughter of mine should go through life called Miss Bubblekins…but the kitten wound her toes in and out, blinked her eyes, mouthed an appreciative meow and the foolish woman became her lifetime slave. That's my girl!*

And Mrs. Stubblefield? Any woman who would wear a tee shirt with her cat's name spread across her pendulous boobs couldn't be all bad. It looked as if…Miss Bubblekins…had scored a reasonably besotted owner, which is, after all, the ultimate goal of any mother and father cat.

"Can I take her today?" Mascara, mixed with happy tears streaked down Mrs. Stubblefield's cheeks. "I'll feed her every two hours and I'll take her to the vet for her shots tomorrow. Please?"

John finally nodded and shook hands with Mrs. Stubblefield. We all kissed the baby good-bye and wished her a happy life.

Within minutes, Mrs. Stubblefield's car shot down the driveway before John could change his mind, the pink carrier shoved in the back seat, and Miss Bubblekins cuddled in her lap.

"I'm so glad things worked out like they did." Black Cat stroked Angel's head with his pink tongue.

Angel put her paws around her babies and dragged them to her heart. "I'm a little sad I didn't have more time to get her on the right track."

Black Cat patted her foot with his paw. "It's our job to give them life, teach them right from wrong, make sure they pay attention to their ancestor's wisdom, and kiss them good-bye. You're staying with me and the kitten has a good home. Do you have any regrets?"

Angel's whiskers twitched "I guess not. Though, I do regret she was named Miss Bubblekins."

Black Cat shrugged his long black fur. "And I do regret calling her cat carrier a whore wagon."

"You didn't!"

"I did, but I have to admit, it was kind of cute, with all the lace and the red ribbons around the door."

Angel looked through the window into the now empty yard where only a moment ago, Mrs. Stubblefield's car had zoomed down the driveway, carrying the baby away forever.

Are those tears in my Angel's eyes? Cats aren't supposed to cry. Maybe I'm wrong. Maybe I'm just looking through my own tears. It's hard to say.

An afterword to this story is on page 240.

50

OBSIDIAN & GOLD

by
Andy McKell

Mariel had ruled the ManyWorlds for time out of mind. But no longer.

Between the worlds lay her domain, now her prison. Through windows that showed many places and many times, she saw the stains of darkness—the sorrows, the silences, the gaps in the sky where there had once been stars.

She was pure in heart; the White Gold Crown had accepted her above all others. She had looked into the hearts of men and recoiled. She had caused their days to be filled with unending light that hid the darkness in their souls.

As eons passed, she craved affection and intimacy, but none could draw near, none could overcome their awe. Her golden aura attracted a worship that was not what she sought, not what her heart cried out for.

She was alone. Too human to be truly Goddess, too powerful to be truly human. This was the price she paid, to be Eternal in a universe that was not. Mariel ached in her solitude.

But the lost Obsidian Crown had found one whose truth was not obscured by the light. Now, there was one not overawed by her, one who could defeat her and lay waste to the peace of the ManyWorlds.

Massed opposing forces had battled on the Great Plain of Stars. Great swathes of time and space had gone forever. Uncounted warriors had fallen; worlds had vanished...and Mariel had lost. Night had fallen across the perpetual daylight of her reign.

She felt him enter the chamber. She did not turn, did not want to look upon his face — the darkness in his heart was already too much to bear. The blood drained from her face, the bile rose and a weakness spread through her limbs. She thrust out an arm to support her weight against the stone wall. His dark aura spoke of the emptiness between the stars, the shadow across her own heart, the great scream of pain between the worlds.

"You know," his voice rumbled in her ears, "your light affects me as much as my lack of it affects you?"

She shuddered, but gave no other response.

"And that is the reason I have not destroyed you."

She spun, color rising to her cheeks. "You cannot destroy me, as I cannot destroy you!" The chamber rang with her hatred and frustration.

"You see? As you weaken me, so your heart is stained with dark emotions. Listen, I feel the ache of solitude and longing in your heart as if I have lived every minute of it. I know this will be me one day—and I do not want it!"

"You have ways to salve your pain." She turned away, seeking solace in her windows.

"No. Devoted worshipers cannot fulfill the deepest human needs."

"Then suffer, as I have! Suffer as the people do. Rule and suffer and be damned!"

"Look at me, Mariel." A simple request in a tired voice.

She turned, glaring and hostile. But something about him had changed, his aura had softened. Could it be fading?

"Mariel, I have thought deeply on this. I wish us to rule together."

She looked into his heart and saw a flicker of light, of warmth, of longing. Never before had Obsidian and Gold stood so close. Never before had two Eternals faced each other.

"The very thought makes me sick."

"As it does me. My stomach churns, my legs weaken, my thinking is unclear."

He grinned, a grin that revealed his weakness, a grin she did not find totally unpleasant, but the realization appalled her.

She felt a touch of sympathy and hated herself for it. "You are new to this. You will darken. Eternity is a long time."

"Then now is the best time for this proposal—before it is too late for me?"

"Proposal?" She gestured wildly, casting vast energies at him, casting him to damnation. She froze. Her efforts had failed, as she knew they would. But she had seen inside herself, seen how darkness had corrupted her light. She stared at her hands with eyes filled with horror. "What am I becoming?"

"Things change. It is their nature. Many of my warriors died at those pure hands of yours. See yourself as you are."

She needed no mirror. She knew already. Her own glow was dimmed. "What have you done to me?" she wailed.

"I have looked into your heart, seen the changes. I know you have looked into mine. Look again. Let us find a peace between us that will spread across the ManyWorlds."

"Never!"

"We can live together or I can hold you captive forever. Either way, your golden days of cloying, perpetual happiness are over. Accept a twilight where we live in harmony, in compromise, in balance. Or we shall both live alone and in pain—my ruling darkness corrupted by shafts of light and your light cut through with darkness.

"You ask too great a sacrifice."

"Have you not already sacrificed too much? Buried yourself inside your duty and your pain? Is there not a time when even an Eternal can rest?" He gestured. "Do none of your windows show how it could be? You know there can be no other for you."

"You know my heart too well."

"As you know mine."

She did know his heart. He needed her light more than any other person did.

She needed the peace from her comfortless labors that he offered. She drew closer, until her white gown touched his black armor.

And as a great twilight fell across the ManyWorlds, those worlds slipped their connection from each other; they fell apart, each with its own human cargo. Some of the people were drawn to the light and others to the dark, but it was the path of their own choosing.

And the twilight endured forever.

An afterword to this story is on page 211.

51

VIEW

by
Mike Boggia

Amara looked through the fortress tower window across the snowcapped mountain peaks and she sighed. Late autumn's frosty wind trees were stripped naked, leaving scraggly skeletal branches thrashing in the gale. She wrapped her wool cape tight, crossed the room past the blazing brazier, and peered at the small city hugging the fortress walls.

In the square, shopkeepers opened their small stores. Peasants drove cattle and sheep to pastures, praying the snows might hold off for another month. If it didn't snow, they would have enough hay to last through the winter. Several men, leading oxen and horses, climbed the hillside into the forest seeking firewood. The animals walked hunched, trying to turn their backs to the wind.

As wife of the fortress commander, Legate Gaius Ferax, Amara held a position of prestige. She looked beyond the city wall and let her gaze follow the road skirting the river. Three days ago, Gaius and his troops rode south to restore order. Raiders from a neighboring province attacked a town, taking livestock and winter supplies. Gaius would force them to surrender the booty. She sighed. The day of his return was uncertain.

Amara, stop fretting, she berated herself. *You are safe and, warm. The fortress and city have abundant food, grain and hay stacked to the rafters. With an extra cohort of troops guarding us, we are safe.* She shivered despite of the warmth of the room.

I wish I weren't so friendless. Most women fear me, only a few will speak to me. Even when Gaius is here, I'm alone while he is busy with his duties. She picked up a narrow silver circlet. *He brought this trinket for me from one of his campaigns. Why do I need a crown? I'm not an empress, though Gaius treats me with love and respect. What I really need is. . .*

A bellow interrupted her thoughts, focusing her attention on the square. She noticed an urchin who drew water from the well several times a day for a blacksmith named Asellus. The child paused, stared up at her for a full minuet, turned, and lowered the bucket into the well. Huddled against the stones, she waited as the receptacle filled. Asellus shouted at her to hurry.

She cast a quick glance at the window, lifted the heavy vessel, and spilled water over herself. Asellus roared several oaths and struck the girl as she staggered through the doorway.

Amara lifted the hem of her robe, raced downstairs and swept past the guards at the portico. Without slowing, she crossed the square and barged into the blacksmith's shop.

The child stood sobbing beside the forge as she pumped the bellows. The glowing coals accentuated a bright red mark on her left cheek.

Amara stood, fists on hips, glaring at the smith. "How dare you strike a child?"

The broad-shouldered man crossed his muscular arms and scowled. "I treat my slaves as I please."

Amara drew several coins for the bag at her waist. "I am buying your slave." She slammed the silver on his workbench scooped up the frail emaciated body. "Legate Ferax will speak to you upon his return."

Two soldiers had followed her. They stood at the doorway, grasping the hilts of their swords. The blacksmith opened and shut his mouth without a sound.

In the warmth of her quarters, she bathed the girl, shocked by her scarred body. Once wrapped in a warm blanket, Amara placed bread and thick wheat cereal before her. The child's timid smile unfettered the chains of loneliness gripping her heart.

"You are safe, little one. We shall adopt you and no one will ever hurt you again." She reached for the crown and placed it on the child's head. "I name you, Gemma, jewel of my life."

Gemma placed her arms around Amara's neck and snuggled against her breast. For the first time in her young life, she felt love.

An afterword to this story is on page 216.

RED RISING

by
Randy Dutton

Beyond Trump Station's thick metallic glass, billions of glittering points streaked past. From the casino's observation deck, Veronica's emerald eyes refocused on an arriving Trojan-class asteroid mining ship. Its blue retrorockets flared periodically, slowing the ship and helping it coordinate its trajectory with that of the geosynchronous spaceport, connected to Earth by a 36,000-kilometer carbon tether. As she watched, Trump Station's gantry crane extended to the ultra-large ship.

The young woman never tired watching the ebb and flow of merchants and Space Command cruisers, and imagined herself someday, traveling across the heavens in total control of her destiny.

A middle-aged man approached the dancer lounging near the window. He slowed to admire both images. Nearest him, her wavy, copper-colored hair flowed over bare shoulders down to a low-back sequined bottle-green costume. A meter beyond, the window mirrored her curvaceous figure, sanguine expression and, just above, a ring of chandelier lights. To him, no one deserved a crown more. She was the most beautiful woman he had ever met, and the most ambitious.

Her eyes shifted to the reflection of the man who had befriended her two years earlier, when she first rode up Earth's premier space elevator.

"Hi, Scotty," she said calmly.

"Miss Veronica, da boss man, 'e say 'ur shift 'es in ten minutes."

Her torso twisted toward him. "Thanks. Have you heard anything?"

His eyes crinkled. "Aye, me lady. The Vestas be a small NEO-class miner arrivin' 'et 2300."

"Any good candidates?" A thin brow lifted.

He nodded excitedly as his stubby fingers passed a memory stick. "'Ere be da data on its crew."

"How long have the men been out?"

"Six mont's."

"And their leave?"

"Twenty days."

"Good.... I'll review it on my next break." Veronica stood and her slender hands smoothed the sexy outfit's wrinkles.

The man's eyes rose to watch her slip a fingernail-sized device into the edge of a plunging neckline.

Veronica's smile widened. Despite the dwarf's years laboring around beautiful dancers, cocktail waitresses, and casino dealers, her beauty still mesmerized him.

Hours later, heads turned from the blackjack table as the long-legged dancer glided past.

"McFears, a word please." Veronica's tone was officious but kind.

"Aye, Miss."

Leading Scotty behind the slot machines, she slipped him a note. "You know what to do."

"Here, sir. I 'ava table for you." The dwarf pulled a stage-center, front-table chair out for the swarthy Vestas captain and replaced the reserved placard with a bottle of rum.

The dance routine commenced and for the next hour, the large man's eyes fixated on the tall redhead in front and, it seemed, dancing only for him.

An afterword to this story is on page 241.

53

ALICE'S ALMOST ADVENTURE

by

Rebecca Lacy

It was a lovely autumn day. A warm wind blew, making the leaves dance playfully as squirrels darted about collecting acorns. Alice couldn't understand why her mother had forbidden her to venture out on such a glorious day. Why should a few sniffles keep her confined to her room? Even Kitten looked sad at the idea of being kept indoors.

Now, Alice is a good girl, who carefully obeys almost all of her mother's wishes. However, even the best of girls sometimes misbehave, and that is just what Alice did on that particular November day.

"Dear me, Kitten," she exclaimed, "why should we stay cooped up in this stuffy old house when there is a world full of adventure awaiting us outside? Suppose you and I slipped out the window and went to play for a while. Surely Mother is too busy in the kitchen to notice our absence. We won't be gone long, then we can return before she is any the wiser."

With the decision made, Alice opened the window, careful not to make a noise that might alert her mother to her plans. She then climbed through, followed by her tiny companion.

Whether it's a looking glass or a window, the oddest sort of occurrences tend to happen to Alice when she climbs through things. Moments earlier, when the child had peered outside, Alice had seen a delightful fall landscape – one that she could draw with her eyes closed so familiar was it to her. In addition to the lovely old oak where Father had hung her swing, there was the white picket fence, and the last of autumn's flowers in the bed Mother kept so well-tended. Of course there was the manicured lawn that was dotted with orange and gold leaves, which Kitten loved chase. It had been there only moments earlier. However, now that she was on the other side of the window, it was all gone. Kitten wanted none of this new development, and quickly hopped back leaving Alice to experience her adventures alone.

Except for the window, which was hanging unattached in mid-air, there was nothing to be seen in any direction. It was as though she was standing in the middle of a cloud. "What a strange place this is," she said aloud even though there was no one to hear her. Or so she thought.

"What's so strange about it?"

Alice looked around, but still did not see anyone who might have asked the question. Shrugging, she began to walk away in search of adventure.

"Ouch! Quit walking on me."

Alice, being quite familiar with strangeness after her adventures in Wonderland, was not taken aback by this as you and I might have been. Instead, she stopped and politely asked, "Where are you? I can't see anything except a cloud."

"Exactly!"

"Exactly what?"

"I am the cloud, and when you walk on me it hurts."

"So, how am I to walk anywhere and not step on you?" asked the perplexed girl.

"You aren't."

"I'm not what?"

"You are not to walk anywhere. You are to simply stand where you are."

"Silly. That would be a very dull adventure, don't you think?"

"Just stand still like a good girl and everything will be cleared up once the vote has been taken."

"What vote? What will clear up?"

The disembodied voice sighed in exasperation, and said "Why should I explain anything to you? Who do you think you are to deserve an explanation from me?"

"I'm Alice."

"Alice? *The* Alice?"

"Since I'm the only Alice here, I guess I am *the* Alice."

"This cannot be! You should not be here. You should be there!"

"Where is there?"

"Well, certainly not here! You must hurry."

"Where am I going?"

"To the Council meeting, of course. A vote cannot be taken until everyone is present."

"I don't understand…"

"There was a terrible fight – all the queens were there. What a mess! There were heads rolling, and poisoned apples, and Maleficent turning into a dragon – she's such a drama queen. Oh, and those awful monkeys from Oz. It was a nightmare, I can assure you."

"That's terrible! What happened?"

"They're dead. They killed one another. Now there is no more happily ever after."

"What do you mean no more happily ever after?"

The voice snickered at Alice's naivety. "Surely you realize, my dear Alice, that unless there is an evil queen to overcome, there simply cannot be a happily ever after. Now you must hurry."

"Why do I have to be there?"

"Why, child, you are the representative for Wonderland. You will be joined by Dorothy, Cinderella, Aurora, and Snow White and the others to decide who will wear the crowns of the departed queens. Oh, and please consider the Knave of Hearts as the Queen of Wonderland. I think he will be perfect!"

"But…oh, never mind. Which way do I go to get to the council meeting? Shall I go to the right or to the left? Or shall I go straight ahead?"

"Tsk, tsk! You may not go any of these directions. You must know that it would be highly undignified for you to arrive through a window. Therefore, you must return the way you came and come back through the looking glass."

Filled with anticipation of a grand adventure, Alice waved goodbye and climbed through the window returning to her own cozy room. There sitting on her bed was Alice's mother, looking none too happy. Without saying a work to the child, she crossed the room and stuck her head out the window.

"Thank you, Cloud. You can go now."

She then turned to a surprised Alice saying, "You see Daughter, you aren't the only one who has had adventures. If you wish to be naughty, you will find that I have more than a few tricks up my sleeve."

An afterword to this story is on page 229.

AFTERWORD: STORIES 1 & 45

Joyce Shaughnessy
author of
THE BLESSING WAY
and
THE EMPEROR

I have really enjoyed being a part of the 750 story thread, where I have found a friendly and supportive group of like-minded authors with whom I truly enjoy the process of writing.

When a story about Global Warming was introduced, I knew I had to write about the forest fires on the beautiful American Indian reservations located around Ruidoso and Cloudcroft, New Mexico. *The Blessing Way* tells the story of a yenene or shaman who is believed to have inherited the gift of healing.

West Texas, where I live, and New Mexico, are both victims of Global Warming. We have suffered severe droughts for years. We have announcements of "fire danger alerts" almost daily.

The story, *The Emperor,* is about Emperor Hirohito before and during WWII. I published three historical fiction books about WWII, so I know about the subject. I chose to write this story because the monthly theme was about ambition. To me, his figure represents the worst when ambition and imperialistic aggression are allowed to flourish.

AFTERWORD: STORIES 2 & 32

Tom Russell
author of
FLYING LIBERTY
and
THE CROWN

It was truly a blessing to work with the Fiction Writers Guild. As a journalist, it has been a challenge to write in an environment that brings me from one style to the next; this is most gratifying. The contributions and critiques from the writers are heartfelt and help in making us better at our craft.

I want to acknowledge and thank Heather Marie Schuldt for all her effort and care in establishing a place we feel comfortable and welcome. Thank you very much. And, to all the writers, you are all truly wonderful, talented, and are generous in sharing your imagination and experience.

Flying Liberty is one of adapting. Throughout history, the notion, and struggle, of survival is reflected in the beauty all around us. Despite the many natural, and increasingly man-made changes to our environment, there is hope. It becomes our responsibility to exist.

AFTERWORD: STORIES 3 & 50

Andy McKell
author of
IN OTHER HANDS
and
OBSIDIAN & GOLD

While working on a series of short abduction science fiction stories, I saw the opportunity to submit to this anthology and almost immediately, the hint of an outline of a story began to form. The theme of Global Warming and my residual thinking blended together to inspire a tale of hope when the future down here on spaceship Earth seems dark and gloomy. However, I don't think we should wait for someone else to fix the planet for us.

Contest-based anthologies provide a splendid opportunity to showcase a wide range of writers and their storytelling. Many thanks to Heather and her erudite and efficient editorial team for a steady flow of splendid collections.

I do hope the readers will find these interesting!

AFTERWORD: STORIES 4 & 27

Todd Folstad
author of
ALPHA LAMPUS
and
THE PREMIER OF WONDERLOVE

Working within the framework of the Fiction Writers Guild and the Writers 750 groups is a great way to have unlocked the newer parts of my writing background. By taking part in these contests, I've used it as a version of "forced writing" to make me work, even when the flow isn't going. All of the stories that I've composed for these monthly events are helping me to hone my craft, exposing me to fresh reads and tools that I may never have uncovered without being able to read the offerings of the other writers.

I'd like to thank Heather Marie Schuldt for her support and control of this "herd of cats" on a monthly basis. She is an exceptionally talented author who gives of her precious writing time to edit and organize these threads for all of the writers in both groups.

AFTERWORD: STORIES 5 & 38

Randall Lemon
author of
TAKING LIBERTIES
and
HEAVY HANGS THE HEAD

Things fall apart. For Humpty Dumpty, his personal tragedy could not be solved, not even by all the King's horses and all the King's men. Today, we face the problem of a possible apocalypse brought on by global warming. Can we rely on our leaders (kings) to solve this problem or will we have to seek our own creative solutions?

In *Heavy Hangs the Head,* a mother and son must make some hard decisions to save the people who rely on them. Sometimes, despite what Mel Brooks might say, it's not so "good to be the king."

In *Taking Liberties*, a much lighter tale, Barbie tries to find a "logical" way to solve the problem of global warming which she fears she may have caused. She finally lights on a solution that is extremely rational from her point of view.

Enjoy!

AFTERWORD: STORIES 6 & 34

Sylvia Stein
author of

A VERY UNUSUAL DAY
and

FOR THE LOVE OF VASHTI

Since joining the 750 group two years ago, I have been able to work with the founder of this amazing group. Heather Marie Schuldt has been such a blessing in my life, and I consider this group of talented writers my friends.

When Heather started the group, she asked the writers if we would be interested in submitting our stories to an anthology and since then we have four Anthologies on Amazon. I have to say it has been a dream come true.

A Very Unusual Day is about a young woman named Amanda who, with her boyfriend, Leo, has to face the fact that there is a major natural disaster forming. They have to pack up and move on if they want to survive.

My second story in the anthology, *For the Love of Vashti*, is about one king who is in love with a beautiful maiden, but her heart belongs to someone else. Both men decide to do what is best for her.

AFTERWORD: STORY 7

Arlene Lagos
author of
WEST OF LUCKY

West of Lucky is about superstition and how it can cause someone to manifest things that aren't really there. Clearly, the main character clings to her superstition as a way of life, which prevents her from seeing what's really happening around her. In a way, superstition and religion does the same thing if taken too far. People do all sorts of crazy things in the name of religion and belief. I wanted to take her beliefs and show how quickly they can turn fantastical. Just as you get sucked into thinking that her world is normal or can be easily explained...you are taken back to the actual reality and reminded of how easily a strong misguided belief can point your car in the direction of crazy town.

AFTERWORD: STORIES 8 & 51

Mike Boggia
author of
ST. JOHN'S LILY
and
VIEW

St. John's Lily is an adaption of my mother's adventures as a little girl. She, her sister, and three brothers sneaked to grandmother's house to see if the devil actually would come to steal the golden blossom from the St. John's lily. I enjoyed the story and wanted to share it. It was a gentler time when children could safely sneak to visit their grandparents, accompanied by their faithful dog, even in the middle of the night.

View was written on a cloudy, rainy day as a spin off from a novel I am writing.

Writing "flash fiction," as these short stories are called, is a challenge and hones my talent. A learning experience with a terrific group of top-notch writers helps make me a better writer. I hope everyone who reads all these stories enjoys them.

AFTERWORD: STORY 9

Glenda Reynolds
author of
WORLD NET UTOPIA

It has been a privilege to contribute to the writing contests at the Writers Fiction Guild and ultimately the Giant Tales anthologies. I applaud all of you who make these things happen. I drew my inspiration for the November Crowns challenge from current sci-fi flicks as well as some political overtones of our present day. If the human race is to survive a nuclear war, what would the government's role be? Would the world fall into a one-government mommy state? And what woman wouldn't want her grumpy husband, after a long day at work, to be able to relax and get reprogrammed with a little help from the Dome (crown)? This was a fun story to do.

AFTERWORD: STORY 10

J. R. O'Neill
author of
WHAT? WHEN? WHERE?

I would like say "thank you" for reading *What? When? Where?* I was inspired to write this story as I was sweltering in the mid-summer Florida climate with an air conditioner that was on the fritz. I tried to tell the story in a way that would show how some of us take the most important person in our life for granted. The fictional J.R. learned what the real J.R. had learned a long time ago. Love, cherish, and appreciate those around you…before it is too late.

AFTERWORD: STORIES 11 & 30

H. M. Schuldt
author of
MIDNIGHT SURPRISE
and
SUNSET CROWN

At times it can be humorous to see how people can easily make a wrong conclusion about complex issues such as creatures from another world and global warming. In *Midnight Surprise*, a woman's intellect has become a snare, so she wrongly discerns that global warming has to do with unexplained warm pockets of air. In contrast, two children, Jessie and Liam, have a much better ability to believe in the Moon Man although they do not understand the facts about global warming, and apparently neither does Jessie's mother. In this fantasy world, two children hang onto what they know to be true even when an adult tries to give them an incorrect description of global warming.

In *Sunset Crown*, you jump right into a light science fiction, slight fantasy future where Kelly and Dan's neighborhood has been destroyed by machines and aliens. This story has action and adventure in a world where an enchanted crown is a tool that can give them guidance in the midst of a world that is falling apart.

AFTERWORD: STORIES 12 & 43

Gene Hilgreen
author of

HOUSE ON THE EDGE OF TIME
and

EMMA IN WONDERLAND

The Writers 750 group run by Heather Schuldt was a Godsend to me. It gave me the chance to hone my writing skills while interacting with other members, who are now like family, on a wide range of topics.

It also gave me the chance to experiment, have some fun, and put my favorite characters from my Buck Axele Davidssen series in situations that matched the monthly short story criteria. Behind the scene, situations happened that would never occur in one of my novels.

The *House on the Edge of Time* was my first attempt at Horror and definitely not one of my better works. But *Emma in Wonderland* took one of my favorite characters — a quantum physicist and downright hottie, and put her in an interesting predicament.

Enjoy!

AFTERWORD: STORIES 13 & 44

Mirta Oliva
author of
THE GREEN INVISIBLE MOUNTAIN
and
IN PURSUIT OF A DWARF PLANET

Aside from having published a children's book and a novel with poems, I love writing short stories. I have written several during the past few months and, so far, one was chosen to be a part of a recently published anthology, *GIANT TALES ~ World of Pirates*. The latter is the third in a series. By following the anthologies' guidelines, I have been able to use the divergent themes as a creative means to broaden my horizons. I was pleased to see my under 3,000-word fiction pieces chosen for several anthologies to be launched at different intervals.

The genre of *The Green Invisible Mountain* can be described as a little bit of fantasy, mystery, Sci-Fi and thriller. The tranquil, while productive lives of a young couple, are suddenly disturbed by mysterious happenings at their farm, such as significant weather changes, disappearing and reappearing acts, and extraterrestrial activities. However, the end-result has a big welcoming surprise.

AFTERWORD: STORIES 14 & 25

Alli Vaughan
author of
SACK
and
FORSAKE THY BLOODLINE

Life is a journey and one to take lightly, lest one become too serious. *Forsake They Bloodline* was a chance for me as a new writer to be a little silly (imaginative) but still confront some serious topics. The story was based loosely on a 1992 Japanese animation named *Green Legend Ran*. In the anime, strange silver-haired maidens are nearly worshiped, but also gravely misused by the powers of their world. Rather than describe a victim, I wanted a story that gave the silver-haired more power over their fate and thus this story came to be. Every moment is just another chance, a chance to change our fate and it is in capturing that one moment, we can become who we were destined to be. My main character does just that and I am sincerely proud of her.

AFTERWORD: STORIES 15 & 35

Lynette White
author of
THE SACRIFICE
and
REBEL KING

My passion for fantasy and mythology drove *The Sacrifice*. Like every story I write, I seek to provoke a thought or a lesson.

How many of us look into the innocent eyes of our children, and somehow, we just know they are bound to do great things? Is our child preordained to do those great things and we are mere stewards? Or do we just believe it enough that we set their course? This question has been debated through the ages.

My thoughts, however, focused on the sweet mother, Anglica. With her faith shaken, she turned to the one person she thought would guide her. Instead, she was forced to make a decision no mother should have to. Does she sacrifice her child to the greater good or keep her for herself? Is it Anglica's tears, or innocent Liberty's, that cause the raindrops in their homeland? The reader must decide.

AFTERWORD: STORIES 16 & 26

Connie Flanagan
author of
THE ENCHANTRESS
and
MORE THAN JUST WINDOW DRESSING

It has been a great pleasure to work with Heather Schuldt and the authors in the Fiction Writer's Guild. The challenge posed by trying to write a short story including certain elements each month keeps me thinking and writing. I am also assured of getting excellent feedback from a wonderful group of writers.

The main character in *More Than Just Window Dressing* is essentially me, and I can't overstate how much I hate shopping, especially for formal wear. So while the specific daydream in this story was created to include the necessary highlights of that month's story contest, the situation of my woolgathering while shopping for something to wear to my sister's wedding, is real.

The Enchantress, on the other hand, is based on a dream I had, modified to incorporate the elements required for that month's contest.

AFTERWORD: STORIES 17 & 48

Neil Carroll Ellison
author of
FOUR SHADOWING
and
TALKIN' ABOUT MY DEFENSTRATION

Windows and crowns and queens, oh my! My goal for *Talkin' About My Defenestration* was to create misdirection. The setup intentionally implies that the queen is a witch. (Which maybe she is—I'll never tell.) When she is forcefully grounded, no pun intended, the story turns into a Monty Pythonesque comedy contrasting modern Ren-fests and free enterprise commercialism with good ol' fashioned rebellion. Oh, and I LOVE the word *defenestration*. Any story with a window should include defenestration. Go ahead, look it up. Great word.

Four Shadowing is the story of a man named Jimmy. What's his world like? In his world, if you step on a crack, you really do break your mama's back. But to be kind, what if the size of the crack determined the severity of her injury? Tiny fissures would equate to minor pangs of discomfort while larger separations would cause longer-term problems. With careful stepping, you could prevent hurting your mother. But accidents do happen. This is the issue facing our main character. He's accidentally stepped on a relatively small defect in his mother's driveway. Not a good way to start a visit to the quintessential American home on the hottest day of the year.

AFTERWORD: STORIES 18 & 31

D C Mills
author of
ALL IN A DAY'S WORK
and
WINDOW ON THE WORLD

Once a month, the challenge is set: a theme, 3 highlights, 750 words. Sometimes, a story just presents itself, begging to be written. At other times, it takes a bit more work. Or a lot. But every single month, I have fun crafting a short story to fit within the parameters – and at least as much fun seeing what everyone else in the group has done, how vast a range of stories can spring from the same small set of prompts.

Being part of a friendly short story group is a constant source of inspiration, support, and I am grateful for it.

My contribution to this anthology consists of the first-ever story I wrote for this group, which was *All in a Day's Work*. *Window on the World* was heavily influenced by the NaNoWriMo project I was working on that month (November 2013). Both stories feature women who have to work with the circumstances they are given, and find ways to cope with difficulties.

AFTERWORD: STORIES 19 & 28

David Russell
author of
IN THE COOLER
and
DECK FIFTY-TWO

I was a youngster during the early 1960s when TV offered animations like *The Jetsons, Rockie and the Flying Squirrel,* and *The Flinstones.* The setting for my story is a convenience store cooler where — like those cartoon shows of the 1960's, the bottled refreshments would sporadically comment among themselves about their current lives.

I am new at the craft of short story writing and am thankful to Heather Schuldt for providing this opportunity to any who are game enough to give it a try it and to other storytellers for their time and encouragement along the way.

I am also thankful to the people who read our stories. I hope they are entertaining, intriguing, and perhaps uplifting.

AFTERWORD: STORIES 20 & 53

Rebecca Lacy
author of
SUMMER MAGIC
and
ALICE'S ALMOST ADVENTURE

I dedicate *Summer Magic* to my mom who taught me to love cloud watching on long, hot summer days. In fact, some of my earliest memories are of lying in the grass, pointing out the different creatures that passed overhead. I still believe that there is magic in those clouds if one is willing to see it. I hope I never grow up and forget.

Alice's Almost Adventure is about my good friend Alice Liddell. She and I became close when Susan Goldberg and I wrote a leadership fable, *Leadership in Wonderland*, which features Alice and her company of interesting characters. I love how she is always up for adventure!

I hope you enjoy reading these stories as much as I did writing them!

AFTERWORD: STORY 21

Karen Beck
author of
SHADOW CHILDREN

Writing is a quiet occupation, usually done in isolation. To take words written to oneself and distribute those words to the world is no easy journey, but the path is made easier when good friends walk with you.

With that in mind, I want to thank my good friends at Fiction Writers Guild for walking this path with me. Their stories, talent, and companionship have inspired me, and made me realize I do not journey alone. To have *Shadow Children* published is a dream realized, but to have it published in a volume alongside so many wonderfully written stories makes this plodding little wordsmith feel like an author.

If you are a writer longing for kindred spirits, or simply someone who longs to hear the echo of other feet on the same path, I invite you to join the writers at Fiction Writers Guild. We would love to have you walk the path with us. Trust me. Good company always makes the journey so much better.

AFTERWORD: STORIES 22 & 47

Shelly Heskett Harris
author of
THE INVITATION
and
FAIR'S FAIR AT COUNTY FAIR

My first novel, *Beyond the Shimmer Gate*, was a fantasy including the magic world of gnomes. The entrance to this kingdom is a shimmer gate. It is natural for my story to be built around the little people.

For thirty-five years I made my living as a journalist, however, fiction was where my heart was. After I retired, I sought out like-minded writers and I was over joyed to find the 750 Club (Writers750), which is both challenging and supportive.

My stories, at least for now, will have the flavor of South Texas where I live.

Few competitions bring out the emotions more than a small town queen contest. A flat bed wagon pulled up in the rodeo arena makes a fine stage for the young ladies in their ball gowns and boots. *Fair's Fair at the County Fair* paints a picture of the competition.

AFTERWORD: STORIES 23 & 42

Lynn Johnston
author of
FORTUNE COOKIE SURPRISE
and
CASSIE'S CROWN

I felt inspired to write *Fortune Cookie Surprise* because I thought of actually writing a book about that topic. In my thoughts, I would have a group of people meet at a Chinese restaurant with every character receiving a fortune cookie. Whatever the fortune said would serve to be that character's fate; it was each person's desire to fulfill the fantasy that made it come true.

I wrote *Cassie's Crown,* because I wanted to write a sweet, heart-warming story that would be perfect for Thanksgiving. Since a crown was chosen as a topic, I decided that the main character would need to feel special because of the crown or its perceived powers.

I am a full-time teacher who teaches kindergarten. I sometimes give my children story starters to help them learn how to write. I thought of giving my children fortune cookie slips and having each one write a story about that topic. I love helping children use their imagination, as I practice stretching mine. Writing competitively has become quite the challenge. Fortunately, it's a challenge that can only help me grow.

AFTERWORD: STORIES 24 & 46

Mary Agrusa
author of
OZ REVISTED
(AN INTERGALACTIC SUBDIVISION ODYSSEY)
and

EVEN STEVEN

What if the tornado that struck Auntie Em's house didn't deposit it in Oz but launched Dorothy, Toto and Auntie Em into orbit in an animated cartoon galaxy? What if they found themselves at the mercy of a young animator under a deadline to produce a story? What if their lives were now governed by the images he drew in each storyboards panel? *Oz Revisited* takes an updated look at an old classic story with a twist. How or will the travelers aboard SS Auntie Em ever return to Kansas? Hop aboard and take a trip with our reluctant travelers as they discover a world unlike any they've ever known.

AFTERWORD: STORY 29

Karen Hopkins
author of
WATCHER IN THE PLAZA

I have spent many years in Mexico and Latin America. My interest and experience in these areas is often reflected in my writing. In addition to short storied, I have published five novels and two stories for children as ebooks on Amazon. My novel, *Shaman Priest,* is set in Guatemala during the turbulent years of the civil war. Three novels, *Down the Colorado, Sparrow Hawk,* and *Up the Devil's Highway,* are political thrillers featuring Maggie and Kiko Perez. The fifth novel, *Monster Slayer's Son,* is set on the Navajo Reservation where I have lived for several years. A sixth novel currently under production is also set on the Navajo Reservation.

AFTERWORD: STORY 33

A.A. Abbott
author of
AFTER THE FLOOD

I live in Bristol, England, a city that hums with creativity. I've always made up stories, even before I could write them down. As well as short stories, I write thrillers set in the corporate world, using the pen name A.A. Abbott. I hope it would encourage more readers to buy my books, on the premise that I also write action. Actually, I'm just a girl with a big imagination.

AFTERWORD: STORY 36

Craig Teal
author of
THE CROWN OF THORNS

I was born in Doncaster in 1979. I discovered my love for fantasy and monsters at an early age after watching *The Clash of the Titans* and *Jason and the Argonauts*, before being introduced to *The Hobbit*.

My love of fantasy, horror and science fiction blossomed over the years until I finally decided to realise my lifelong ambition of writing and producing fantasy games and stories by setting up my own business, Composite Games Limited.

My first story, *The Crown of Thorns,* was written with my Occult Tales game setting in mind, which is currently targeted for a 2015 release following the release of my epic fantasy game, *The Chronicles of Ollundra.*

AFTERWORD: STORY 37

Shae Hamrick
author of
RAIN

After learning of the premise for the November short story, I settled on a queen from one of my previous stories who was trying to decide what to do next. She really wanted all of her trouble in the past to just melt away like ice in the storm. The rain falling outside her castle window in the cold early spring seemed appropriate for her struggles. Then it was just a matter of seeing where she went next. I particularly enjoyed writing this story, as it has so many interactions between Marissa and the setting around her.

Hope you enjoyed the story!

AFTERWORD: STORY 40

Victor J. M. Christensen
author of
THE JIĂGŬ CROWN

I am very fond of writing; I enjoy being part of the group and being able to read, and learn from the talented writers in it. It's a fantastic opportunity, which I'm very grateful for.

My story, *The Jiăgŭ Crown,* is a story I've been considering for a while, and which I might build further upon in the future. The primary focus of the story is what dreams really might be, because dreams really are difficult to understand, I find them really fascinating. What explanation might there be when you experience an event which seem really familiar? Perhaps you feel like you know what's going to happen next? Perhaps dreams are a key to knowing the future?

AFTERWORD: STORY 41

Tim Girard
author of
WHY WE FLY

It has been a pleasure working with a group of talented writers and editors. Heather challenges us each month with a new subject. The challenge of writing a story limited to 750 to 1000 words is a learning experience I've found helpful in writing my novels. I find inspiration everywhere, from people watching, working outdoors, news articles, then let them run around my brain and formulate a story. Different genres interest me and I enjoy exploring the possibilities in a variety of short stories.

AFTERWORD: STORY 49

Elaine Faber
author of
MISS BUBBLEKINS

Miss Bubblekins was a condensed, edited scene from my novel, *Black Cat and Angel's Journey*. Creating a stand-alone story from a novel is a challenge. Limiting the tale to 1000 words is a double challenge. Through the Fiction Writer's Guild, our skills are tested, writing stories with specific criteria. November's story had to include *a crown, a strong woman, and a window*.

In the story, *Miss Bubblekins*, we get inside Black Cat's head as he is about to lose his family. Paralleling human emotions, we see through the cat's eyes, his rage, despair and finally acceptance that his family will be better off without him. And we experience his inexplicable joy when the situation changes.

My own cats have inspired many short stories, published in magazines and anthologies. The first of my Cat Mystery series, *Black Cat's Legacy*, was published in 2014.

AFTERWORD: STORY 52

Randy Dutton
author of
RED RISING

Red Rising begins the journey of a female pirate, Veronica. It's a story I felt compelled to write after having published, *The Red Lady*, a 'space-based' pirate story about a woman with charm and beauty rivaled only by her ambition. Some characters beg to have the whole story told.

www.ingramcontent.com/pod-product-compliance
Lightning Source LLC
Chambersburg PA
CBHW050025180626
46810CB00002B/577